Hoops of Steel

A Novel

Marion Goldstein

D1523815

Also by Marion Goldstein

Hard to Place

Embracing the Sign

Architecture of the Unpronounced

Author's Note

This is a work of fiction. Names, characters, places, and incidents are products of the author's imagination or are used fictitiously and are not to be construed as real. Any resemblance to actual events, locales, organizations, or persons, living or dead is purely coincidental.

Acknowledgments

I wish to thank the many people who shepherded this book to completion. To my editor Kathryn Liebowitz, whose sensitive, careful editing illuminated my blind spots. To my children, who read more revisions of the manuscript than a mother has the right to ask for. To my friends, who were my early readers and offered their time and honest critiques; Pauline Burt, Wendy Dolber, Marty Milner, Linda Morgan, Elin Mueller, and Dena Uribe Olsen. And to Joe Ofria who created and designed the cover, my heartfelt thanks.

In Memory of Elizabeth Michael Boyle, O.P.

You were
The gentle force
Sprinkled like salt
Over everyone you met
Drawing from each
Our own luster
And giving back
All we didn't know we lost.

Those friends thou hast, and their adoption tried,
Grapple them to thy soul with hoops of steel…

~ William Shakespeare, *Hamlet*

Prologue

2012

It was before seven and still dark on that February morning in 2012. The first fingers of light had not yet opened the new day. The early hour caused Margo to lunge for the phone as its ring broke the silence.

"Yes?"

There was a hesitation, as if the caller was deciding whether to speak or hang up, and then, "Hello, Maar-go?"

A sliver of memory—the voice, the pregnant pause; her heart leapt in her chest.

Angela? Could it be? She had long hoped for a call, some reaching out, some sign that Angela and Lou were ready to talk about the events of that long ago December when everything started to go bad. The passage of time had eradicated all expectations. Over the past thirteen years she had cobbled together different fantasies to explain the estrangement. There had been an incident. More than a decade had gone by and her anger, intense in those early months, eventually hardened like stale bread.

1

The last evidence of friendship was the Christmas card that came in 2000. Angela had written, "Dearest Margo and Kevin," the same salutation she'd used the previous thirty years. It seemed to imply affection. Since that card, only silence spoke until the phone rang that morning.

Part One

Chapter One

1996

The busboy cleared the breadbasket and empty bowls of pasta from the white linen tablecloth. Frank Sinatra crooned in the background and a candle in its amber glass globe flickered in the middle of the table. They had ordered espresso when Lou, bantering with the waiter as was his custom, waved his right hand over the table, and said, "A piece of Italian cheesecake, with extra whipped cream and four forks for my friends here." It was a spring night in 1996. Angela and Lou, Kevin and Margo were finishing their bi-monthly dinner at Lunello, a restaurant in Hillsdale, New Jersey. The four of them had dubbed it the "halfway restaurant" because it was midway between their homes, Lou and Angela in south Jersey and Kevin and Margo in the northwest part of the state. Without traffic, it took about an hour for each couple to get there; with traffic, it took Kevin and Margo closer to two hours while Angela and Lou's backroad route remained one.

From where she sat, Margo glimpsed the wall of Italian landscapes. Mario, the owner, had transferred them from his old place, and over the years the two couples had been meeting, she never tired of looking at them. The evening was winding down, a signal for the friends to consult calendars and attempt to plan their next dinner. Lou took the lead as he reached into his breast pocket for his appointment book. He didn't open it but placed it on the table. He shifted his large frame forward in his chair. With the little boy voice and sheepish look that Margo had long associated with his rare moments of nervousness, he said, "I have something I want to ask you both."

The body knows and releases chemicals into the bloodstream that bloom into a hive of excitement. It is only in retrospect that the mind has reason to parse that moment, destined to play itself out – for good or for ill. There is a before and there is an after. This was one of those moments.

"Sounds mysterious," Margo joked, secretly excited, thinking perhaps Lou and Angela were considering another trip and would propose a cruise or a tour, like the one they took to London and Paris a few years earlier. Something big to anticipate. Lou hesitated, as the waiter returned with a huge wedge of cheesecake topped with strawberries and mounds of whipped cream. With a flourish he placed it on the table, along with a fork for each of them.

"It's about your son."

"Our son?

"Which son?" Kevin and Margo asked in unison.

"Finn. I want to bring your son, Finn, into my operation."

"Really? To do some consulting?" Kevin asked.

"No, much more than that. I want to offer him a job." With a conspiratorial glance at Angela, Lou said "I'd like to bring him on to help me take the business public, and groom him to succeed me when I retire."

Kevin and Margo were stunned, their forks full of cheesecake poised midair. Kevin reacted first.

"Take it public? That's a big move. I knew business was good, but not that good," Kevin put down his fork and did a quick calculation in his head. "How many years since you started PARC Labs, fifteen, sixteen?"

"Right," Lou said. "We are in our sixteenth year."

"You've come a long way from that chemistry cutup in a Brooklyn classroom," Kevin said, typical of their camaraderie, playfully reminding them about Lou's run-in with a Bunsen burner that brought the fire department to his high school chemistry lab.

"Well, it's a dream now, but I've made the decision to pursue it. It will involve significant expansion and lots of business development, and it won't happen overnight, but if I don't do it now, I'll never do it."

Margo's eyes met Angela's across the table. She was hanging back in her chair. Margo recognized her anxious habit of placing her right index finger taut above her lip, while her thumb and other fingers rested below her chin, like a small clamp keeping her mouth closed. She wondered if Angela had misgivings.

She had been so excited and bubbly when they started the business. It was the first step in the scaffolding they were building to keep the children close. With the way the business operated, she already had that. She had not yet said anything about Lou's proposal to bring Finn into the company. Margo wondered if her friend was a reluctant participant.

Overlaying all her thoughts was a question, "Why Finn?" It was Kevin who verbalized it.

"Why Finn?"

"He's got the background," Lou answered. "I started thinking about him a couple of years ago when we were visiting you. He was moving things out of his New York apartment to store in his old bedroom. I was in the kitchen getting a bottle of beer when he laid a big cardboard carton on the table, and I asked him what it was. He told me it was a box of *tombstones*."

Ah, the tombstones, Margo thought. Such a funny word for those Lucite pyramid-shaped "memorials" awarded to business analysts and their clients after an initial public offering or after successfully buying, selling, or restructuring a business, in some cases taking them from bankruptcy to solvency. She used to tease him that they were the adult version of a Little League trophy now that he had entered the big league of investment banking.

"Yes, I remember that day," Margo said. "It was shortly before Finn and Audrey got married. He needed to make more room in his New York City apartment." (The tombstones gathered dust in his old attic bedroom ever since, along with his tarnished twenty-year-old trumpet and collection of running shoes he never seemed able to part with, and, of course, his Little League trophies.)

"Well, I couldn't help but notice the engraved names: The La Jolla Hotel Chain, Runnells Lumber, Trainers, Gordons Fresh Market. All major companies. That's when your son first crossed my radar."

"You never mentioned it before,"

"I wanted to be sure before I said anything." Lou confessed, "I've been following Finn's career from afar ever since. Most of what he does is public information. I keep up with trade publications and with whatever I can glean from the internet. I know he has the background to get us ready to be a public company and eventually run the whole enterprise."

Lou's knowledge of Finn's career was a surprise. Like most couples, they were interested in each other's children in a peripheral sort of way, sharing successes, giving and receiving support when one or the other of their offspring was going through something. They had, over the years, talked to their friends about Finn in general terms, but no more so than about their other children, Declan and Maura. Lou knew of Finn's MBA from Stanford and that he was working for a very well-regarded firm.

It was a proud moment for them to learn from Lou that Finn was receiving public recognition in the world of New York finance. At the same time, a ripple of unease coursed through Margo as she considered just what constitutes an invasion of privacy.

Twenty years later, Lou's words about accessing public information would return to her when she sought information about him. Although she told herself her actions were a legitimate perusal of public information, a part of her felt as though she was sneaking around, crossing a boundary and invading Lou's privacy. (She did it anyway.)

"I've given it a lot of thought," Lou continued. "Over the past six months I've been working with a headhunter. I've interviewed a lot of candidates."

"You couldn't find anyone?" Kevin asked.

"Yes and no. They all had something to offer but I couldn't get excited about the long-term prospect of working with any of them."

"Did you interview women?" Kevin asked playfully, having had many discussions with their daughter, Maura, about the conscious and unconscious prejudice women face in the workplace.

"To be honest," Lou said, as he attempted to deflect the question, "I told the headhunter to only send me resumes from men. You know, I don't think a woman would work for the boys."

Kevin, Margo, and Angela howled, knowing Lou's old-fashioned protectiveness towards women, based on his similarly dated assumption that females were less well-equipped than males to take care of themselves. "You sure it's the boys and not you?" Margo teased.

"Well, maybe a little bit," Lou acknowledged, creating a tiny space between the index finger and thumb of his oversized hands.

"What was wrong with the candidates you did interview?" Kevin asked.

Lou hedged, "They were all competent young men, and I got close to making an offer to one of them, a fellow from one of the big investment banks in New York. He had all the qualifications except one."

"What was that?"

"He had no sense of humor. I just got a blank stare with my best material," Lou said as he crossed his eyes in a mocking gesture. "I started thinking, I don't really know this guy. I couldn't get comfortable with the idea of him taking over when I retire. I couldn't wrap my head around a stranger belonging."

"I get it," Kevin said. "I was thrilled when Declan came to work with me. I hope he will still be with the company when I retire."

Margo knew that to be true. It was only five years ago that Kevin had asked their oldest son to leave his job at one of the big six accounting firms and join him in his business. It took Declan a while to make the decision. By then, he was married with two small children. Transitioning from a big, renowned company was a major decision. He finally said "yes," but not before asking Kevin for a contract, unlike his father, who had built the company doing business with a handshake.

Yet it was that attention to detail that made Declan so valuable. Kevin saw himself as a salesman. His satisfaction and joy came from winning a new client, then moving on to the next one. Declan, on the other hand, was a much better administrator, crossing t's and dotting i's, to ensure things ran smoothly.

"Did you ever consider bringing on Maura or Finn?" Angela asked.

"No, they had other interests. It wouldn't have been a good fit for either of them."

Kevin continued, "You have Artie, Rob, and Carl, working with you, Lou. That's always been the dream, no? Why go outside the family?"

"Yes, that's true, and I'm grateful. Don't get me wrong. I love working with my sons. But I've had to face it, although they are each great at what they do, none of my boys have the overall financial and business experience to take PARC Labs to the next level."

Margo could tell from the look Lou gave Angela before he spoke, and the hesitation that preceded that admission, how hard it was for him to admit none of the boys had the same skills and aspirations for themselves as he had wished for them. Finally, as if to rescue Lou, Angela jumped into the conversation, "We brought each of the boys into the company right after college. Perhaps that was our mistake. They never got experience outside of PARC Labs and while they run it beautifully, none of them have the creativity or background to bring in anything new. That's what we need to grow it."

Kevin was still focused on the potential of Lou's sons. "What about Paul? I know he went his own way after college. Any chance you could entice him to join you?"

"No, I've tried. He's settled in his job. But even if he were ready to make the move, he doesn't have the background or interest to eventually run the company."

Kevin persisted. "How about business school for one of the boys now, to prepare him to take over?"

Lou shook his head emphatically. "That ship has sailed. The time for an MBA would have been five to ten years ago, after they got out of college. Believe me, we've discussed it. By the time they got their college diplomas they were done. They weren't interested in any more school, and they still aren't. We all want the business to thrive when I step back. I'm not getting any younger and I figure I will work for maybe another ten years. I need to groom someone for when that day comes. I know the company's potential. But I can't do it by myself. The three boys are as excited as I am about bringing in your son. Finn is as close to family as I can get."

Lou took a breath and then with a look in his eyes that Margo had never seen before said, "I want to learn how to play the piano, I want to write poetry, I don't want to work forever."

The image of Lou plucking away at piano keys or composing a sonnet was not one Margo or Kevin had ever imagined. It took a moment for them to realize he was not joking.

In the brief silence that followed, as they absorbed his sincerity, Lou said, "I would treat Finn as one of my own."

Of all the things he said that night, this one sentence deposited itself in Margo's heart like a gold coin. Who could want more for their child?

Years earlier, when an imminent business trip exacerbated her fear of flying, Margo confided her anxiety to Angela. Picturing her children orphaned due to some vividly imagined plane crash, she convinced Kevin that they needed to make a will naming a guardian for the children.

She called Angela and tentatively asked, "Could we name you and Lou as guardians for the three kids?"

Angela was quick to respond. "Of course, you can name us as guardians in your will, but there's not going to be a plane crash," she reassured. "Nothing's going to happen to you." Then a hesitation as she thought of Maura, who had come to be known as the only petunia in the onion patch of the boys. "But I'm already thinking about what color pink to paint Maura's room."

She made Margo laugh but she never doubted that Angela

and Lou would take care of her children. Now the situation was reversed. The thought of Lou wanting to bring Finn into the inner circle of his family and his business echoed the trust she had felt all those years ago. His coming to them first felt like an old-fashioned marriage proposal, rooted in an Italian culture that was familiar to Lou and Angela but foreign to them. Nonetheless, it engendered a closeness that felt like love.

Chapter Two

1959

Theirs had been a couples' friendship. During the mid-fifties, as teen-agers, Angela and Margo knew each other casually from their Brooklyn neighborhoods. There, lines were drawn according to the parish church you belonged to and the school you attended. Angela was from East New York, Margo from City Line, two adjacent neighborhoods nested among the sixty-five that made up the borough of Brooklyn. Their generation was one where the young adults lived at home until they got married. Their parents remembered the great Depression. Margo's father often returned milk bottles to the grocery store for the five-cent deposit that served as fare for his daily train into Manhattan to his job at a bank. Her mother wore house-dresses and always looked harried. Besides taking care of her four children, she tended to three elderly aunts who lived above them in the gray-shingled two-family house with its red brick stoop.

Angela's father was a city cop, handsome in his navy-blue uniform, badge shining on his chest, nightstick swinging from his belt, as he patrolled the sidewalks of East New York where racial tensions boiled amidst the poverty of the melting pot that was Brooklyn. Her mother started working in an office when Angela, an only child, was ten years old. After school, Angela let herself into their apartment in the Projects, one of the first multi-story apartment complexes to grace Brooklyn. Each evening she listened through the door for the clang of the elevator followed by the click of her mother's high-heels, and the swish of her nylon stockings against her tight skirt as she returned to the apartment from her job as a secretary.

Unlike later generations, Angela and Margo had no formal name to designate their place in society other than "the fifties" generation. They were shy girls who followed unwritten expectations of their local lives: graduate high school, find a job, and contribute to the family until you get married and leave the house for your own tiny apartment, generally in the same neighborhood. There was pressure to marry. To be among the ten percent of "girls" turning twenty-five and still unmarried was to be stigmatized as an "old maid." The exception to the unmarried rule was to have a vocation to a higher calling, such as entering the convent right after high school, and taking vows of poverty, chastity, and obedience in the service of God.

Margo lived on one side of the elevated train line that ran through the East New York section of Brooklyn, Angela on the other. Angela went to public school and wore store-bought clothes, even slacks. There, tight sweaters, and miniskirts were not only permissible but the source of much Catholic school envy. Margo attended Catholic school where slacks were forbidden. A navy-blue jumper, with the school initials embroidered in gold on the shoulder and navy knee socks were the dress code for eight years of grammar school, replaced by a gray plaid pleated skirt and gray knee socks through the four years of high school. Their clothes marked them. They bred trouble, as rivalries flourished and whole student bodies judged each other by their schools, easily identified by the clothes in which they found themselves.

They knew each other casually. During the early fifties, the polio vaccine did not yet exist and a polio epidemic besieged Brooklyn. Angela had an aunt and uncle who lived with their children across the street from Margo's house. When Angela's eight-year-old cousin contracted polio, she and her mother came and spent Saturdays visiting Dottie, who was confined to an iron lung in her house. In the evening Angela joined her healthy cousins and the other kids on the block, including Margo, in games of stoopball or stickball or ringolevio. Neither of them was athletic at twelve-years-old, but Angela, unlike Margo, was never the last one standing when teams were chosen. Being a cousin to those five siblings mattered. Besides Dottie, there was Eddie, Ronnie, Vinny, and Freddie. They took care of each other. Family watched out for family. Margo's siblings, on the other hand, were too young to be included in the street games, and she drifted onto the team with the least number of players. She yearned for a bunch of sturdy cousins to pick her for their team.

Other than those summer nights, when the city streets rang out with the voices of boisterous teens, neither of them had a reason or an impulse to seek each other out. They were white noise buzzing somewhere in each other's background.

WHEN A BLIZZARD CLOSED THE CITY AND ALL ITS BOROUGHS FOR two days in the winter of 1959, all that changed. The lines of demarcation that separated the neighborhood where Margo lived and the neighborhood where Angela lived were buried under five feet of snow. The radio produced nothing but static. Trains didn't run, cars were swallowed in shifting drifts, the shops under the elevated train lines were shuttered.

The snow finally tapered off and the sun burst from behind

the clouds like an invitation to venture outside. They were nine-teen years young and had an unexpected holiday from the subway ride and the three-inch heels they wore all day at their nine-to-five clerical jobs. It was a day for making snow angels, regressing to their twelve-year-old selves with the bonus of tumbling in drifts with their boyfriends, Kevin and Lou, who literally rolled into each other in a snowbank. As Angela and Margo shivered on the sidelines and their lacquered hair turned stringy in the wet, they witnessed the beginning of a friendship,

"Did you play football for St. Thomas More?" Kevin asked Lou. "You look familiar."

"Yes, I did. Did we play against each other?"

"No, I played basketball and baseball at St. Anslem's, but I went to all the football games."

"Did you play in college?" Kevin asked.

"No, I had to work. No time for sports. How about you?"

"Same with me."

They began to bond as they learned they'd each earned a scholarship to their respective high schools, and held one job after another to make the college tuition payments their parents were unable to eke out of household budgets.

Later that day, the scent of wet wool from their damp coats competed with the sweet aroma of chocolate egg creams at Gus's, the only ice cream parlor to open in the blizzard. As Angela and Margo removed their coats and draped their soggy gloves over the radiator hissing the cold from the room, they took each other in. Angela was tall, probably three or four inches taller than Margo's five-five frame. Her short golden blond hair was slicked back from her face in a DA, commonly known as a Duck's Ass. Squared at the base of her neck, the hair met at a part in the center of the back of the head where it was said to resemble a duck's tail. It was the rage haircut of the late fifties. Only a perfect face could get away with such a severe haircut and Angela's face was near perfect. The braces that kept her from smiling as a teen were gone, replaced by a wide smile that emerged slowly as she made eye contact. Her dark eyes, flecked with hazel light, rarely left Lou. Margo could see how much she trusted him. But didn't they all in those innocent days when they were ready to commit their lives to someone before knowing what life was all about?

As they began to settle at the table, Angela looked directly at Margo and said, "Where did all your freckles go?" Margo laughed, remembering how each summer the sun tattooed her with hundreds of freckles that were the bane of her adolescent existence. "I discovered make up," she said, "the freckles are still there and when summer comes, they will bloom again." It took Angela a while to realize the thick glasses Margo had relied on were replaced by contact lenses, but she recognized Margo's long, straight, yellow hair as it tumbled from under the hood of her jacket, exactly the same as when she'd tied it in a ponytail during those street games.

They noticed the engagement rings flashing on each other's fingers. A flurry of "You're engaged. Us too." Followed by the ritual of shared admiration, "Let me see your ring, how beautiful." "Let me see yours, gorgeous." Their mutual admiration gave Kevin and Lou an opportunity to revisit what Lou christened the "diamond run," to describe the previous summer when in addition to a day job, they each worked nights to put the small, promised diamond on their girlfriend's fingers. Their differences dropped away in that red vinyl booth like the ice cascading off the telephone wires and the limbs of maple trees growing along the edges of the concrete sidewalks of City Line. They had planned their weddings for the following June, only a week apart. Such symmetry seemed like kismet.

KEVIN AND LOU DISCOVERED THEIR COMMON HERITAGE AS THEY reminisced about sports, their injuries, and the day in 1957 when the Brooklyn Dodgers won the World Series. But it was mostly their shared sense of humor that drew them to each other. During that glittering afternoon, Gus lost customers through their reluctance to leave the booth for others who were standing not so patiently in line alongside the ice cream counter.

Angela, the only public schooler in the group, asked, "Do we really have to go to those Pre-Cana lectures at church?"

"As far as I know, the church won't marry you unless you attend all six," Margo said, "and they're each five hours long."

"What can an eighty-year-old priest who's never been married possibly teach us?" Lou asked.

Reluctant participants, the four of them signed up for the same six Sundays—Angela and Margo serious, while Kevin and Lou in competition for the humor they could extract from the basement of the church with its makeshift rows of folding chairs and chipped statues of saints staring from dusty alcoves.

There were about fifty couples gathered from all over the Brooklyn dioceses to prepare them for the one and only marriage that would endure *till death do us part*. The room was quiet. This was solemn business. Suddenly the silence was broken and everyone within hearing distance was staring at Lou as he announced, "I had a hard time getting a date for this afternoon."

Not losing a beat, Kevin responded, "Yeah, I had to call five girls before one agreed to join me."

Angela and Margo turned red with embarrassment as the other couples overheard the banter.

For five hours over each of those six Sunday afternoons, they listened to the old priest talking about marriage. Margo and Angela blushed as he delved into the rhythm method, the only Catholic approved plan for birth control. They learned they needed to maintain a Catholic household by abstaining from meat on Fridays, and about the obligation to contribute to the church, to attend Mass on Sunday, and to have their children baptized, sooner rather than later. Margo, Kevin, and Lou were so steeped in Catholic education that to do otherwise would never have occurred to them. It was clear to Margo from observing her friend's relationship over the past few months, that even though some of these Catholic commands were new to Angela, she would acquiesce to whatever rules Lou decided to abide.

The gentle old prelate's every thought was punctuated with the same phrase, "Be nice." Kevin and Lou began counting. "That's one." "That's two." "That's fifteen." "That's twenty-two." Other couples sitting nearby could hear. Some glanced disapprovingly, others, enticed by Lou's infectious laugh, silently joined in the conspiracy of the "be nice" count. Margo, uncomfortable with their foursome being the center of attention, mouthed "stop it." But Kevin and Lou were having too much fun. Having an audience fueled Lou's humor, and in retrospect, was a foreshadowing of many scenes that would take place in years to come as, like the pied piper, Lou's irreverent comments drew strangers to their little group. (They didn't know it then, but the priest's recurring theme of "be nice," would toll like a church bell over the years.)

Their lives were completely overtaken with the prospect of walking down the aisle. The tabula rasa of their futures as brides stretched out before them. For a small fee, Angela and Margo enrolled in Eugenia Shepherd's School for Brides, a program advertised in the *Herald Tribune*. Margo felt so mature, as one night each week, she hastened from her job at the New York Telephone Company, descended into the subway and boarded the A train for Manhattan, to meet Angela. Angela would be waiting for her on the station platform, having just come from her job at a law office Uptown. "Maar-go, over here," would echo above the commuters as the departing train rumbled down the tracks. After threading their arms together to deflect the crowd pouring into the station, they clambered out of the subway. They gobbled hot dogs and orange soda at a street vendor's stand on the corner of Eighth Avenue and 34th Street, then made their way to *Henri Bendel's* and the class on bridesmanship. As they approached the store, they observed well-coiffed debutantes being dropped off in taxis and chauffeured limousines and realized the School for Brides was on the to-do list of the rich and famous in Manhattan society. Girls like them, stenographers and clerks from the borough of Brooklyn, learned about it in the pages of the *Herald Tribune* or in the coffee-break room, where the luckiest were able to garner fifteen minutes, and not a minute more, for themselves during the day.

Eugenia Shepherd was a society and fashion columnist in New York City, famous for setting trends and reporting gossip in her newspaper articles. Barely five feet tall, with a mass of tight yellow curls, she carried herself like the icon she was, the high priestess of inside knowledge when it came to weddings, gossip, and decorating.

When Margo and Angela arrived, assistants were undoing the red velvet ropes cordoning off the dishes and glassware department of Bendel's for the School for Brides being held that evening. A banquet table of finger sandwiches, pastel cookies, and lemonade served as an invitation to nibble, after meandering among the dazzling display of over fifteen fully set tables, each with ten place settings. The white tablecloths and pastel napkins on each table were color coordinated. If there were lavender orchids imprinted on the china, there were fresh flowers in shades of lavender in the centerpiece and lavender napkins fanned out in silver rings on each plate. At least three crystal glasses adorned each dinner plate and a full display of sterling silver utensils: knives on the right, forks on the left, spoons next to the knives—all indelibly etched in their minds that night. Optional, they learned were the little silver name card holders for guests to easily find their place at the table. Angela and Margo listened to conversations around them like spies in a foreign country.

"So, which are you ordering," one young bride-to-be asked another, "the Rosenthal or the Royal Doulton?"

Margo's eyes met Angela's, which seemed to have doubled in size. It was at that moment they realized they were not so much in a school for brides but on a shopping expedition.

"Did you see the price of those dishes?" Margo whispered.

"Oh my God! Who can afford that?" Angela whispered back. "I feel like I'm an extra in a movie."

Terrified of spilling cookie crumbs and lemonade on the pink gauze-draped chairs, they sat in the back of the room. Soon the room quieted as Eugenia Shepherd stood at a podium and addressed the audience. She lectured about Karastan carpets and flocked wallpaper. She recommended covering their couches with the same pattern that they chose for the walls, "to make a statement." She invited questions. A sea of hands, each adorned with a diamond that flashed under the fluorescent bulbs, waved in unison.

"Which is better, fine china or bone china?"

"Bone china."

"How can you tell which is which?"

With a nod of her yellow curls, Eugenia sent her assistant to fetch a plate from one of the tables. She held the plate up to the light. "Just hold it up carefully. If it is translucent, you know it's bone."

Little did Angela and Margo know, as they scribbled in their notebooks, that evaluating the translucence of china would soon be superseded by delicately holding babies to the light to check for diaper rash and cradle cap. When a future bride, memorable in her red felt hat with a feather and white gloves, asked what to do if a guest placed a bottle of beer on the dinner table, Eugenia became apoplectic.

"Never, never. Under no circumstances should a bottle appear on the table."

"Well, no need to write that down. Kevin and Lou aren't going to forgo a beer to accommodate Eugenia Shepherd," Margo whispered.

"What about ketchup?" Angela printed in bold letters on her note pad before placing it before Margo to read.

"Good luck with that," Margo mouthed, as she crossed her eyes to make Angela laugh.

Kevin and Lou met them at ten, under the brown-and-white-striped canopy at the front entrance of the store to accompany them home after each class. The subway cars rumbling from downtown Brooklyn were considered unsafe for women at night. Near empty, they provided vagrants a convenient place to sleep. As the local train labored from one station to the next, Lou and Kevin had endless fun probing for the contents of their notebooks. "So how many different size crystal glasses do we need to buy before we get married? Did you learn how to fold napkins yet? What color paint did Eugenia say we should use in the kitchen?"

Angela and Margo would feign annoyance while stifling their own giggles. They occasionally went so far as to change their seats in the uncrowded train, but not too far away from their gallant protectors. They were trying so hard to be mature as they closed the door on their teen years and leapt into the rest of their lives, with the voice of Eugenia Shepherd following them every time they bought a dish towel or a saltshaker.

What was really happening was so much more. They became a true foursome. Their friendship, like ripples in a pond, expanded, encompassing more and more of their lives.

ALTHOUGH "BE NICE" CONTINUED TO REVERBERATE THROUGH the years, Eugenia Shepherd's advice on decorating and entertaining soon faded. It was replaced by Dr. Spock's bible on colic and eczema and all things baby when, the following year, Angela gave birth to Paulo, who came to be known as Paul, and four months later Margo's first child, Declan, was born. Conversations about how to survive three weeks of rainy weather with a crying baby, choosing a foolproof gate for the top of the stairs, what age to toilet train, and how to steal a few minutes of quiet for themselves, obscured Eugenia Shepherd and her School for Brides.

A year later, Paul and Declan giggled as they threw handfuls of sand at each other across the sand box in Angela and Lou's backyard. Kevin had just assembled wheels for Lou to attach to the red tricycle they were putting together for Paul. "Where do they go, bottom or top?" Lou joked as he held the handlebars upside down to emphasize just how little each of them knew about assembling anything. It was a lazy summer day. Angela was seven months pregnant, embedded in a lawn chair. The grill, sizzling with sweet Italian sausage prompted Margo to urge, "Hurry up, we're starving" as she unwrapped the fresh Italian bread from the bakery bag. Finally, Paul's shiny new red tricycle, its wheels attached firmly, was one more rite of passage in the lives they were constructing. Lou got two beers and two bottles of water from the cooler and nodding towards Angela's ample belly, turned to Kevin, "We would like you to be godfather for the new baby."

Kevin was taken aback. "Really? I thought that was an honor reserved for blood relatives, especially in an Italian family, not some guy you met in a snowstorm."

"You're more than that," Angela chimed in.

Two months later, the baby was born. It was Kevin who stood tall at the baptismal font, the proud godfather, as the priest poured water over the grand mop of black hair of

Angela and Lou's second son, Arturo, who came to be known as Artie. Not to be undone in this race to fulfill their destinies, six months later, Maura, the only girl amidst the two families, was born.

On mild afternoons, Angela and Margo packed the babies and toddlers in a stroller and met on *The Avenue*, that quarter-of-a-mile stretch of stores that ran between their small apartments. They'd stroll, keeping one another company while checking the theater marquee or looking in the windows of the ladies' dress shop, or the economy store, with its packages of underwear in every size that the kids outgrew before they could wear them out. Tucked between Nathan's Bar & Grill and the butcher shop was the antique store, with its ever-changing bargains calling to them through the stained-glass window retrofitted into the front door. This was their favorite place for browsing.

In taste, Angela and Margo gravitated towards the old. Despite Eugenia Shepherd advocating for the new and shiny, they sought out early twentieth-century milk glass and silver soup ladles enshrined in tarnish that could polish to their original luster. There was something endearing about the old, with its silent history of enduring.

As brides, still living in small basement apartments that dotted the older streets of Brooklyn, they dreamed of owning big old houses to "fix up." Angela and Lou found one soon after Arturo was born. While they sunk every extra penny into refurbishing what came to be known as "the money pit," Margo and Kevin found a modest row house with minimum upkeep, built almost a quarter-of-a-century later. Yet the old still attracted, and Margo continued to scour antique shops for the cast iron Dutch oven or cookie jar, or hurricane lamps, newly freed from someone's attic. Together, they mined the crowded tables for treasures, the older it was, the more treasured. This was one of those symmetries of personality they shared. It also encompassed those things they couldn't find in an antique store, like their friendship. The older it grew, the more treasured it became.

"Look at this," Angela said one day as she picked up a maple plaque engraved with a message, *Friendship, A Reason, A Season, A Lifetime.* It reminds me of us."

"I love it, if you don't buy it, I will."

"Finders keepers," Angela teased, as she began the ritual haggling with Bezoza, the custodian of the treasures. Two dollars later, Angela carried it home, cleaned it up and painted it to match her kitchen. Each time Margo visited, she'd see it hanging over the kitchen doorway and feel the warmth of those early days.

She believed their friendship was that of a lifetime. She never questioned it. It was self-evident, the way gravity is self-evident. From that first bonding in the blizzard, through the School for Brides, through rain-drenched mountain honeymoons in forgettable hotels that remained the secret they shared with no one else, through the birth of all the babies. Their friendship evolved into seasons that kept renewing. Its continuation was a foregone conclusion. They were in it for life.

Chapter Three

1996

"We'll give Finn a call," Kevin said to Lou as they all hugged goodbye in the dark outside Lunello. It had started to rain, a spring rain that brings with it the promise of trees bursting into leaf and crocuses emerging from the newly thawed earth. Unlike previous rides home from Lunello, when driving up the Turnpike Margo deferred to the pasta and wine and hum of the wheels to lull her to sleep, that night she couldn't wait to get into the cocoon of the car and discuss what had just happened.

"What do you make of all that?' she asked Kevin as soon as they were alone.

"I knew Lou's business was successful but taking it public? That's a whole other league." Kevin said.

"I know he has over three hundred employees, but I'm stunned he's not counting on one of the boys to take over."

"He's a realist. From what he says, I don't think any of the boys has the background to take PARC Labs where he wants it to go. Finn probably does. Did it surprise you to learn how much Lou knew about what Finn has been up to?"

"It did. I was a little taken aback. I guess what he garnered from his snooping led him to believe Finn has what it takes to lead the company forward," Margo said somewhat sarcastically.

"Think of it as research, not snooping," Kevin said. "It could be good for Finn."

"What about Paul? From all they've told us, he's very successful at the pharmaceutical company where he works."

"Unlike the other three, Paul has outside corporate experience. But it's in sales. That isn't the background needed for preparing a company to go public. Just because one might be the best professor in a school doesn't mean the skills will translate to being the best president of the university."

Margo remembered how disappointed Angela and Lou were after Paul graduated from college and went his own way to work in one of the pharmaceutical companies that were burgeoning in the area. For years they believed he would reconsider.

"I give him two years," Lou had said. As time went on, it changed to "I give him four years, I give him six years," until he finally accepted Paul's need to be independent. Even the promise of a BMW and the down payment on a house didn't entice him.

"Did Angela ever tell you why Paul never came in with them?"

"No, but I had my suspicions," Margo said, as she thought of the time Lou drove to Paul's dorm in Philadelphia during a snowstorm to help him finish a paper. Paul didn't want the help and wouldn't let Lou in. Of course, Lou turned the scene into hilarity when he related it months later, his banging on dorm doors, wet and hungry, until some sleepy-eyed kid let him in. As funny as it was when Lou described that scene, it made Margo wonder about the control coming from Lou, how perhaps it was too much interference for Paul and made him wary of putting himself in a position of having his father as his employer.

They knew Artie, Rob, and Carl had been working at PARC Labs since graduating college. From its creation on the kitchen table of their home in Princeton, this merging of family and business was their dream. It was Lou's insurance policy for his boys' ultimate success and safety in life. He kept the family close, orbiting like planets around him; a powerful sun, controlling the whole enterprise and exerting his influence. If he sensed something amiss with one of his offspring, he stepped in, and Angela deferred to his decision.

They had toured the company a year earlier when Lou threw a party to celebrate its fifteenth anniversary. Located in a sprawling industrial park, the building and the parking lot were flanked by well-tended evergreens and flowering cherry trees, planted when the building was constructed. Initially Lou rented the space, but he had since bought the building. A handsome glass-enclosed sign, installed on the manicured lawn outside the front door read, "PARC Labs."

His three sons worked from large offices flanking Lou's corner office behind the reception area. From her desk in reception, Angela served as the heart of the company, greeting customers, answering phones, and offering her generous personal attention to whoever came through the door. Overflowing plates of homemade Italian cookies, baked at home in her big Viking oven, added to the homey atmosphere surrounding an otherwise modern business. The brass name plates bolted into the doors of each son's office offered a glimpse of their roles: Arturo Romano, Accounts and Sales Manager; Roberto Romano, Production Manager; Carlo Romano, Plant Operations Manager.

"We have over sixty-five-thousand square feet," Lou said as he extended his arms in a sweeping gesture. They were standing on a glassed-in deck, accessed by a steep ladder-type staircase that seemed to float above the lower level which housed the plant equipment. Lou flipped on the lights, illuminating the huge stainless-steel drums that fired the sugar spheres. A second series lit up the warehouse, where products were packaged, taken to a loading dock, and shipped to myriad pharmaceutical companies.

"You done good," Margo told Lou after taking in the shiny brass plates that spoke of his pride in his sons and the state-of-the-art facilities gleaming before them. "You and Angela are living your dream."

"We are. Never thought we'd get to this point," Lou said as he rolled his eyes towards Artie's office door.

Every family has their black sheep, and over the years Artie held that position. He was the gregarious star quarterback on his high school football team and with that came parties, drinking, and girls. This earned him another year of prep school at Lou's insistence, before he went to college. There were a few hiccups in college that resulted in his graduating in five years instead of four. Now Artie was settled in the business, the father of a little boy, and happily married to a "good woman," who according to Lou, spends "more time with her horses than with him," which was an ongoing source of amusement in the family lore. Of all the children, it was Artie who most resembled his father, the same girth, and the same way of pronouncing certain words, that wasn't quite a lisp, but rather a charming idiosyncratic sound.

Two years younger than Artie, Rob radiated quiet when he walked into a room. Rob seemed to have earned the most generous portion of Lou's confidence. Handsome, well over six feet tall, with a head of black hair, he was married and lived in a mini-mansion two miles from his parents, with his wife, Rose, and two daughters. From what Margo could gather, the proximity of their homes was both good news and bad news. There were occasional references to Rose resisting the ritual dinner

Angela prepared each Sunday, or Rose "sulking in the corner." Nothing serious, more like an occasional weed in an otherwise manicured life.

Their youngest son, Carl, was less involved in the day-to-day running of the business. His degree was in architecture, not chemistry, as Lou had hoped. "I wouldn't have been surprised if he was the one who refused to work for us," Angela once confided. "Lou convinced him there was a spot, what with adding new buildings and redesigning space as the company grows. We manage to keep him busy enough."

Lou had his own unique way of describing his youngest unmarried son. "Sometimes I look at him and think, where did you come from? He wears clothing from Barney's and shoes from Saks. He looks like he belongs on a fashion runway instead of a factory floor. But he's happy with his new BMW each year and the old Victorian house he's restoring."

The family vacationed together, renting a big house on Rehoboth Beach each July. All the boys joined them, with their wives and children, for at least a week. One September, when they met at Lunello, Angela joyfully described the caravan of BMW's, packed with beach chairs, umbrellas, and grandchildren headed for vacation. "We looked like a band of gypsies on the run."

"I'm jealous," Margo said, envying her friend's ability to keep the family around her.

"I know how lucky I am," Angela said with a contented sigh.

But Margo knew it was more than luck, as was the plan to invite Finn into the inner sanctum.

THEY TALKED FOR A GOOD FORTY MILES ON THE DRIVE HOME, leaving Edison and Plainfield in the rearview mirror. "This could be a huge opportunity for Finn," Margo said to Kevin, "to leave Manhattan and the long weeks of travel and fourteen-hour workdays for the relaxed culture of Lou's business, with no corporate bureaucracy to navigate. What could be better than that?"

Margo had always been fascinated with how people drift in and out of your life and influence it in ways never dreamed of or anticipated. Mesmerized by the road unspooling in the glare of headlights, a scene wafted into her consciousness. It was a summer Sunday in the early seventies. They were spending the day at Angela and Lou's first house in Brooklyn, the infamous "money pit." The above-ground swimming pool in the yard lured the children from the moment they arrived. Each found a corner of the house to change into their bathing suits. Angela and Lou's sons were olive-skinned with mops of dark curly hair. The three Conroy children had fair skin that crisped in the sun. When Finn, at six years old, appeared at the top of the stairs wearing only his bathing trunks and his enthusiasm, Lou took one look at his skinny white body and joked, "Why, he looks like a glass of milk!" Everyone laughed except Finn, confused by the attention, and Margo, as she suddenly saw her son through her chemist PHD friend's eyes. Her mind flew to anemia, then leapt to leukemia and froze there. The day was spoiled for her as she worried about her pale son splashing in the pool. The following morning, she took him to the doctor to have his blood checked. He was fine. However, the fear that Lou engendered is something she never forgot. Now, decades later, Lou was ready to entrust his business, and by extension his family, to the skinny glass of milk wearing his brother's hand-me-down swim trunks all those years ago.

Finally, all talked out, that sense of contentment that comes from a good evening with old friends, and the joy of hearing accolades heaped on one of her children took over and Margo dozed off.

SHE COULDN'T WAIT TO CALL FINN THE NEXT MORNING. KEVIN convinced her to hold off until Monday and let him have his Sunday without thinking of work.

She reached him in the office at eight on Monday. "We saw the Romano's Saturday night. You'll never guess what we talked about."

Hearing the excitement in his mother's voice, he laughed and said, "Sounds like you're going to tell me."

"Well, Lou implied, no he told us, he is looking for someone to take over his company when he retires. He wants to talk to you."

"Me? Don't his sons work with him? Why would he want to talk to me?"

She explained the Saturday night conversation at Lunello.

"Why didn't he just call me directly."

That was a good question. Having taken so much pleasure in the proposal the night before, it was a question Kevin and Margo hadn't asked themselves. Now that it was posed, she mused, "Maybe he was feeling us out, finding out if we knew of any plans you already had that would preclude his reaching out."

"He still could have called me directly?"

"I think he just wanted to let us know how much he thought of you, make us proud, or maybe it comes from his Italian heritage."

"What do you mean?"

"I'm sure he got Angela's father's permission to marry her, and I suspect he has raised his boys to do the same before they got engaged." She could sense how foreign this sounded to Finn. After all, it was a job offer they were talking about, not a marriage.

"Maybe he just really wants to recruit you and thought we would use our influence." This, of course, is exactly what she was doing, having already decided how great this would be for her son.

Finn listened and when she finished said, "I've got to tell you, at business school I took a class called the Perils of a Family-Owned Business. There are a lot of reasons why it's not a good idea, and it's not something I ever thought about pursuing."

"But it sounds like such a perfect fit for you."

"Family businesses are risky for so many reasons, Mom. Bringing in an outsider can create a whirlpool of issues. Boundaries blur and business communication can become bogged in family drama that spills into the office. History is full of case studies where, despite their best intentions, when the time draws near, owners are just not able to let go of the reins and turn over their creation to an outsider."

"But Lou's not like that. He doesn't see you as an outsider," she said as her heady thought, that she had stumbled upon a diamond-in-the-mine of career opportunities, began to evaporate.

Finn hesitated "Okay. I'll talk to him if you would like me to."

As she listened to his far less than enthusiastic reply, she realized he was being polite. His mother was asking him to do something for a friend. Finn put it in the same category as if she were asking him to drive his grandmother to the doctor in a snowstorm or use his influence to get coveted tickets for a World Series game for his father. He would save them the awkwardness of explaining his disinterest to Lou.

"You've nothing to lose. It's only a phone call," she urged, as her excitement waned, and she realized he wasn't interested. He was doing her a favor. But then, he was always accommodating.

The youngest of three children, Finn was a happy, easy-going kid who eventually grew into the role of peacemaker among his siblings. From the time he was a baby, he was always on the move, escaping playpens and backyard fences and awkward moments. He often startled her and made her laugh at his observations. One that remained with her was his last day of third grade: She heard the screen door bang as he ran into the kitchen, shirttails streaming, cheeks flushed, report card in hand, and blurted out, "Mom, you want me to be a nice average kid, right?"

"Sure."

"Good, I got all C's on my report card. I'm average."

And he was off with a handful of lettuce to feed his rabbit in the backyard hutch. Evidently, he had taken himself out of academic competition with his sister, who fretted over getting A's.

Average continued to be his friend for the next few years. Then in sixth grade, just before the move to junior high, he met a teacher, who through some alchemy in the classroom, changed everything. Finn suddenly became his sister, working to achieve nothing less than an A through seventh and eighth grade and into high school.

Midway through his freshman year, Margo got a startling phone call. "This is Mrs. Green, I'm the admissions officer at the Cranford Willoughby School." Margo knew of this private school by way of its reputation. It was within walking distance of their house and some of her neighbors' children attended it.

"Yes?"

"I'm calling to tell you that I just spent an hour with your son Finn." She listened. "He took it upon himself to stop by and express interest in transferring to CW from his current high school. He just left my office."

"Finn?" She was totally baffled. She wondered if this Mrs. Green had dialed the wrong number.

Sensing Margo's confusion, she continued, "he told me you didn't know his plan to change schools and I told him that, of course, I would be calling you. This is a first for me. Never in all my twenty-two years as the admission officer has a student come in on their own to inquire about admission."

Margo didn't know whether to laugh or cry. She thought she knew everything that was going on with all her children, but this was not even on her radar. "What did he tell you?" she asked.

"He said he sometimes gets bored in school. He has some friends who are taking subjects like Latin and Advanced Math here at WC, courses that he thinks will challenge him but are not offered in his current school. He also told me he feels like his older sister and brother's friends, who I gather are juniors and seniors, tease him at school and it makes him uncomfortable."

"I had no idea," Margo confessed to Mrs. Green, who continued, "I know WC is an expensive school, and of course, he would have to take a test before we could admit him, but I wanted to make you and your husband aware of your son's visit. Please let me know if you would like me to arrange to have him tested."

A half hour later she heard the unmistakable sound of Finn, running as usual, up the driveway before banging into the kitchen. She stopped preparing dinner and looked at him expectantly as he opened the refrigerator door and poured himself a glass of chocolate milk.

He still hadn't met her eye. She waited a minute in silence. Nothing. Finally, "So? What's going on? Do you have something to tell me?"

And it all came tumbling out —"... the teachers are always comparing me to Declan because he's so popular and good at sports, and to Maura because she's so smart, and I want to run on the track team but I have no way of getting home after practice because I have to get driven to and from school on Declan and Maura's schedule and I'm always around their friends and I feel *like a baby* and my friends Eric and Gary get to do so many great things at their school, and could I please change schools and go to CW with Eric and Gary?"

It wasn't easy but they found a way to send their secret student to the school of his choice. It was an investment they never regretted. For the next twenty years he worked as hard as anyone as he made his way through high school, college, graduate school and, finally, the career he'd carved out for himself. Always self-motivated, he made all the right decisions for himself.

Margo was sure this would be no different. He would take the time to tactfully tell Lou that he wasn't interested in his offer. He would save his parents the awkwardness of explaining, secondhand, their son's lack of enthusiasm and ultimate rejection of their friends offer. She had no doubt that Lou and Angela would understand. This almost merging of their families would be relegated to the repertoire of family stories they would continue to tell and tell again. She could only imagine how Lou would turn it into a comedy.

Chapter Four

1960s

"There are no more cartoons," Declan whimpered from where he and Maura sat cross-legged in their flannel footsie pajamas, mesmerized by Bugs Bunny, as with a fizzle the picture disappeared from the tv screen and the house went dark. Guided by some innate mommy radar, they flew through the newly darkened rooms to the kitchen where Margo was peeling potatoes to add to a casserole ready to slip into the oven. She had just put Finn, their third child, only two months old, down for what she hoped would be a couple of hours, during which time they could have dinner. Kevin was on his way home from work. She expected him somewhere around seven. He had started a new job at an accounting firm in New Jersey six months earlier. The added responsibility earned him a higher salary, something they sorely needed with an infant and two toddlers under four years old. The extra money was a tradeoff for the long commute to New Jersey.

That all changed the day the house went dark. November 9, 1965. Margo scooped up a crying Maura and held Declan's hand as she made her way to the window. Even the streetlamps were out. As she rummaged through the junk draw for a flash-light the phone rang. It was Angela.

"You, okay? Is Kevin home yet?

"No, he's probably on his way. Do you have lights?"

"No one does. We have a transistor radio and just heard that the entire Northeast is without power. There's a blackout covering eight states and the provinces of Ontario and Quebec in Canada."

"Oh boy. That means Kevin is probably caught in this too." She did a quick calculation of where he might be. Probably in a subway car under the Hudson River. Anxiety rose in her chest just as Maura whimpered, "Where's Daddy. I want to see him."

Angela heard the whimpering over the phone line. "You want me to send Lou over later to help you get the kids to bed?"

"I think I'll be okay. I'll call you if I need help. Let me hang up just in case Kevin is trying to call me."

But there was no call. Margo stared at the phone all night long, willing it to ring. She wrung her hands and prayed as she fantasized about his train moored under the Hudson River, packed with commuters who had no way of extricating them-selves. From there her imagination rampaged—to a mugging on one of the darkened city streets that were, even then, an incubator of civil unrest, or a stampede of frightened travelers, or a fall onto the third rail of the train tracks.

Finn awoke hungry three times during the night. Holding his little warm body close in the dark, as the formula and sucking lulled him back to sleep, got her through till daylight. It wasn't until eleven the next morning that she heard the key in the door. Her vigil ended. It had been almost thirty hours since Kevin left the house for work the previous morning.

She learned his train had indeed been brought to a sudden halt somewhere between New York and New Jersey, in the Hudson Tubes, that three-mile stretch of tracks embedded

ninety-seven feet below the Hudson River. There was no stampede, no mugging. Around two that morning the police and fire
department arrived, having descended onto the tracks, and
walked almost a mile in the darkened tunnel to where the train
was stalled. They methodically climbed aboard, rescued the
now cheering commuters and led the little platoon peacefully
along the tracks to the nearest station. The passengers climbed
the stairs into the blackness of city streets, said goodbye to the
people they'd shared their exile with, and were on their own to
patch together a route through Manhattan and Brooklyn to
reach their respective homes.

"Why didn't you call me?"

"I thought you'd be asleep, or I'd wake the kids. Besides the
phone lines went round the block and I didn't want to waste the
time waiting," he said as Maura and Declan abandoned their
toys and jumped into his arms, screeching "Daddy's home,
daddy's home." The decision to move, to leave their little
rowhouse in Brooklyn, was made that week. Within six months
they had packed up their lives, said a sad goodbye to the old
neighborhood and left Brooklyn, although in truth, Brooklyn
never left them.

In the months preceding the move, Angela and Margo
made all sorts of promises about not letting the shift in geog-
raphy change their friendship. Prominent among the promises
was, "Every Fourth of July, no matter, we will continue to spend
it together," as they settled on the national holiday to anchor
the friendship with a standing date pinned on their calendars.

AFTER MARGO AND KEVIN MOVED, AND WHILE THE CHILDREN
were young, it was easier to keep those promises and maintain
the close friendship. As young mothers tied to a routine of children, they spoke on the phone at least once a week. They desig-
nated a time. When the babies were down for a nap after

lunch, even if colic or an earache made a nap impossible, they tried to keep their promise to each other, as they entertained the sleep abstainer with one hand and held the telephone receiver with the other.

By the time the children were in school, their phone calls dwindled to snatching a few minutes every other Tuesday morning. After the back door banged with the last child's departure, the residue of Cheerios floating in bowls was dumped in the sink and the requisite snitching of the last pancake or swirl of scrambled eggs left on a plate was swallowed, one of them would dial the phone.

"Are they gone yet?"

"Just left."

They would put up their feet in respective kitchens and take fifteen minutes for themselves, working out solutions for how much time to allow the kids to watch tv, how to handle recurring sore throats, worries over money, or classroom bullies, before jumping into the shower to begin the rest of their day.

Soon Angela became pregnant with their fourth child, Carl. She devised an age-related key to keep track of her four boys in the hierarchy of oldest to youngest. PARC for Paulo, Arturo, Roberto, and Carlo.

Within the first year, it became clear the distance between their homes worked against the small things they had shared: afternoons with the kids at the park, the occasional Avon or Tupperware party when they got a night out, Saturday afternoons when Kevin and Lou helped each other assemble a swing set or basketball hoop while sharing a few beers in the backyard. It added up to a big loss.

Their lives diverged like kites in the wind. While living in proximity they had made appointments with the same gynecologist to deliver their babies, and the same pediatrician to care for them. They frequented the same playground, the one where the sand was replaced and kept clean, the same shoe salesman who really knew how to measure the kid's feet. They shared which barber to avoid, the drug store that sold Pedialyte and stayed open all night for the fevers that spiked, the small things that go into daily life for which they needed each other. Their promises about staying connected, like boxes of stale cereal, became outdated without their realizing it. New friends populated their lives and became their everyday confidantes. Yet, always in the background, they all believed the foursome would hold, a bedrock to return to, regardless of when their last conversation took place.

DURING THOSE YEARS, THE WOMEN'S MOVEMENT THAT BEGAN IN the sixties was fermenting around them. Angela and Margo were too busy to really take notice, changing diapers and reading *The Little Engine That Could* to toddlers, while coaxing their seven-year-olds to eat vegetables instead of jellybeans. Kevin and Lou both narrowly escaped the draft lottery that was scooping up younger men and sending them to fight an unpopular war in Vietnam. While anti-war rallies and riots erupted on university campuses and city streets as protests surged, they remained on the periphery, tucked in the nests they were building. For women, pregnancy was synonymous with giving notice to leave your job. There was no daycare or maternity leave, or any of the social structures fought for by the women who came after them. Expected to quit their clerical jobs before giving birth, Angela and Margo conformed. They each worked until eight-and one-half months pregnant, before "retiring" at twenty-three to begin the next stage of life as homemakers, the way their mothers had. Their lives and their aspirations were local.

They were fulfilling their vocation of motherhood. They had chosen this life, were living their dreams. They had their children, their homes, their husbands. Yet something not quite palpable was missing.

As the sixties ended, the woman's movement gained traction. Still in their provincial world, Angela and Margo never read *The Feminine Mystique*, never joined an organization that confronted their lives beyond the Parent Teachers Association. If they had been exposed to the "tyranny of domesticity" as put forth by the new feminists, they would have laughed at the notion. Creative urges were centered on decorating their homes or sewing drapes or maternity dresses. They loved their lives, small as they were, orbiting around their households and the children who completely depended on them. Although they never doubted their roles as mothers, there was a gradual amorphous yearning for more. With it came the shame of not being satisfied with all they were accumulating; washing machines and dryers and dishwashers and cars, the accoutrements of the middle class, designed to liberate the homemaker. The realization that there was a world beyond their homes was a gradual revelation.

Like many women who married young and began their families in the sixties, they found themselves in a world of routine. They whined on the phone to each other in a lighthearted way. "There's got to be more than getting the kids off to school, making beds, doing laundry, fixing lunch, fixing dinner, overseeing homework, monitoring tv, bath time, bedtime, only to get up the next morning and start all over again."

Peggy Lee's popular song "Is That All There Is" put a name to what Margo, more so than Angela, couldn't yet confront. The refrain was spinning in her head one snowy February morning as she vacuumed and dusted and folded the laundry. Angela called all excited.

"You won't believe it, Margo. I got a part-time job."

"You're kidding? Where?"

"Do you remember the butcher shop between the Economy store and the candy store?"

"Yes, where we always stopped by for free lollipops."

"Well, the butcher died, and a children's clothing store took over the location. It's called The Little Girl's Boutique. I'm having so much fun with ruffled socks and pink eyelet dresses after all the drab jeans and corduroy pants and cotton shirts that have been my life. Getting out of the house, having some adult conversation…you wouldn't believe."

"How are you managing with the four kids still so young?"

"My parents are helping. My father drives my mother over just about every day to give me a hand."

"You sound happy."

"I am. I'm earning money that will help when and if, pray God, Lou opens his own business. It's so great to feel like I'm contributing. Besides, just being with other adults a few hours a week makes such a difference in my mood."

Angela had found a way to fulfill herself while working towards her and Lou's dream for the future. Margo was inspired by Angela's bold move. She would get a job too. Perhaps that would alleviate her sense of purposelessness. She became an Avon Lady, selling products door-to-door for about six months. While Maura and Declan were in school, Finn would hold her hand and accompany her as she rang doorbell after doorbell with her catalogue and samples of lotions and creams. Initially, she had a goal. A sale made her happy, opening the boxes of beautiful products that customers ordered was satisfying, delivering the products, and earning her own money bolstered her self-esteem. Yet, it was a temporary fix. It failed to fill the emptiness that was gnawing at her heart.

MARGO HAD YEARNED FOR ANOTHER CHILD, BUT THAT WASN'T happening. What did happen was something she lived in fear of and never thought she could survive, the death of her fourth child twelve hours after his birth. In her eighth month, one moment she was peering at the little bulges in her abdomen, cupping her hand over a fist or foot making itself known to her. The next, standing horrified over a pool of warm water bursting from her body, the beginning of the end. She knew in the days and months that followed, she would never be pregnant again, could never go through this falling in love with a child growing inside her, only to have him snatched away. This sorrow morphed into a clinical depression. Without babies, which she saw as her contribution to the world, who was she?

As the long winter turned to spring, she continued to flounder. Her peers, her neighbors, the mothers on the playground or in the PTA all seemed content. What was wrong with her?

It was Kevin who finally said, "Why don't you talk to someone?"

"You mean a therapist?"

She was terrified. She was ashamed. She had everything she wanted: children she loved beyond words, a home she loved, a husband she loved. Yet she was miserable. Each day she would make the beds, pick up toys, do the laundry, make breakfast, lunch, and dinner, all the while, ruminating about what her life was all about. She thought she was going insane. The stigma attached to psychological help was embedded in the culture of the time. She didn't know anyone who saw a therapist or even how to differentiate between a psychiatrist, a psychologist, and a therapist. To *talk to someone* implied mental illness and mental illness was hidden, never talked about, and reserved for those who were consigned to mental institutions or electric shock treatments.

She told one person, her next-door neighbor, Marie. While the older children played street hockey in the driveway after school, Finn, and Marie's youngest, Brian, were consigned to the fenced backyard where they constructed cardboard tracks for Matchbox cars or amused themselves with chasing the family rabbit. Margo and Marie would share a cup of tea in the late afternoon, in the hour or so they had before they cooked dinner. In many ways Marie become another Angela in Margo's life.

It was Marie who was there for her the day the dam broke and Margo sat at the kitchen table, unable to stop crying as she confessed her sense of despair.

She didn't know where to begin to find the help she needed. Kevin who must have been listening to the "be nice" priest almost ten years earlier, suggested he contact the old cleric and explain the situation. Within ten minutes of doing so, Kevin had the name of the psychologist who would help Margo get her life back. Week after week, month after month, Marie minded Finn those mornings Declan and Maura were in school, and Margo went to her therapy appointment.

The therapist, a clinical psychologist, worked from his home several towns away. That suited Margo fine since she didn't want to be seen going into his office, wary of being labeled a mental patient. His diagnosis was clinical depression. "It will take a year before you feel better, but you will climb out of this," he assured her. A year seemed like an eternity. She didn't know how she would get through. Initially the doctor saw her three times a week. Somehow, during those sessions, he normalized some of her symptoms when he told her "There is a generation of women like you, who lack a community in which to grow as they take care of their families and maintain a home. You are not alone." He did not think she was insane. He thought he could help her work her way out of depression.

In that first year of therapy, he teased from her a long-forgotten high school memory. She had requested her guidance counselor transfer her out of the academic track for the home economics track. Sister Mary Loretto fought her, saying over and over, "You are college material." Her words must have lodged in Margo's psyche, the way seeds dispersed by the wind in a field will someday take root. This simple four-word sentence uttered a decade ago, was a key to unlocking the depression that was stealing her joy. Over several sessions, the story unraveled. How as an eighth grader she'd been invited to take the entrance exams for Trinity Academy, an all-girls scholarship school, shining like a beacon in downtown Brooklyn, drawing girls from grammar schools all over the borough. When six weeks later, she sat in her alphabetically assigned seat among sixty classmates, she was prepared to be disappointed when Sister Annunciata read the admission list to Trinity. There were four girls listed in alphabetical order and "Margo Weighton" was the last name on the list. She was in.

It wasn't easy, those hours spent navigating the three over-crowded rush-hour trains each day to and from downtown Brooklyn, plus the balancing act of trying to master Latin, Spanish, algebra, and physics. At the end of sophomore year, a choice was offered to all students. Continue the academic tract or switch to a less demanding commercial tract, where the focus was on typing and stenography in preparation for a job as a secretary, or the even less challenging home economics track offering sewing and cooking in preparation for becoming a homemaker.

The reality was, Margo couldn't see beyond her mother's life—raising a family and taking care of her home. Her mother's present was Margo's future. She asked herself how the more rigorous academics would make any difference to her life? On a more conscious level, she fantasized the new clothes she would create in a sewing class, how she would wear them to parties, on dates. Sister Mary Loretto reluctantly gave her what she wanted. Her lectures on how Latin and physics would prepare her for college, and how college would prepare her for life, evaporated as soon as Margo stepped out of that windowless office, tucked into the basement of that classically constructed stone building.

It wasn't until graduation was upon her that she revisited her decision. In May, the class was awarded a weekend bus trip to Washington, D.C., overseen by the nuns. She had never travelled further than New Jersey, and it was with a spirit of adventure that she packed for the weekend. They visited the Washington Monument and the Lincoln and Jefferson Memorial, the National Gallery, the Air and Space Museum, the Tomb of the Unknown Soldier, and finally Annapolis where smiling midshipmen posed for pictures with the gaggle of girls descending from the buses.

After the photos, Margo, and her best high school friend Barbara, tucked their knees modestly under their pencil skirts and nylon stockings and lowered themselves onto a grassy knoll on the campus. Neither of them had ever visited a college campus before. There was something about that spring day, the cherry blossoms blooming above them like a cloud of possibilities, the monuments full of history, the smiling students carrying their books into their dorms.

"Did you ever think about waiting to get married and going to college instead?" Barbara mused, as they girl-talked over their dixie cups of ice cream.

"I'm thinking of it at this very moment." Margo gushed— shocking herself as a new idea took its place alongside the long-held goal of getting a job and saving money to get married to Kevin after he graduated from college. "Sometimes I wonder what going to college would be like. I know it's expensive and if anyone goes to college in my family it will be my brother."

"My two brothers are in college now, studying engineering," Barbara added. "But there's no money for me to attend either."

"If you could go to college, would you study to be a nurse or a teacher?"

"I guess a teacher," Margo said, "since biology lab made me faint."

"Yes, I remember you keeling over and falling into one of the nuns when we had to dissect a frog."

They dared to dream that afternoon, intoxicated by all they were experiencing, wondering out loud about an alternate future. "Let's talk to Sr. Mary Loretto when we get back to school."

They never did. That idyllic day of sharing their amorphous thoughts ended. The following day they rode the bus back to Brooklyn and climbed onto the roller coaster to graduation. But something must have shifted in Margo. A few months later, after getting a job at the New York Telephone Company, she learned the company would pay college tuition for employees. A hastily constructed addition of Quonset huts had been added to St. John's University, to accommodate Vietnam vets returning from the war. Not quite the dorm experience she had briefly dreamed about on that trip to Washington, these Quonset huts consisted of huge, curved steel ribs for the frame and an outer shell of corrugated metal. They housed the classrooms. The location was a short walk from her job in downtown Brooklyn. She gathered her courage and enrolled knowing she would find herself in night school classes with veterans and a few young women like herself. She attended classes two nights a week while earning and saving money during the day. Her wedding was still her priority.

It was no small thing, retrieving these memories in psychotherapy. Sister Mary Loretto's words had evidently landed on fertile ground. They had lain dormant inside her until this mental health crisis unmoored them. Like so many women of that generation, their development stymied when they forfeited an undergraduate degree for marriage, Margo rediscovered a goal she barely remembered having.

Yet, with three children, returning to school seemed an

impossible task. Angela joined Kevin in encouraging her. "Take one course at a time."

"It will take forever."

"So what?" Angela replied, as she helped Margo see how the timing didn't matter, reminding her, "You'll be doing something for yourself, something that will make you happy.

College can be your job, look how happy my job makes me," she said.

Margo took the plunge and enrolled in evening classes at a local college, a decision that changed her life. Kevin saw to dinner and put the children to bed on the nights she had class. When she got home at ten, the house was quiet. Kevin would turn off the ballgame and listen as she pulled out her notes and revisited the world that was opening to her. Slowly, as the psychologist predicted, slivers of joy began to filter through the depression.

Chapter Five

1970s

"It's so hot, when are we going to get there," was the chorus coming from the back of the unairconditioned car as Margo and Kevin drove through Manhattan to Brooklyn. It was the Fourth of July, and Kevin was trying to skirt his way around the New York parade as they made their way to their touchstone date, a barbecue with Angela and Lou and their four boys.

Declan, Maura, and Finn joined the Romano kids in the pool within minutes of their arrival. The four adults sat nearby, cooling off with cold drinks, when there was a commotion in the pool. In an outburst of exuberance, Carl had scooped up a red plastic pail full of white pebbles, recently installed along the driveway to keep mud from accumulating. He tossed them willy-nilly into the pool, barely missing the other children playing in the water. Artie bounded from the pool to chase his brother, who by this time was screaming," Mommy, mommy, Artie is trying to get me." Angela sorted out what happened, as they all peered at the stones freckling the bottom of the pool.

Lou, who was wearing shorts, took off his shoes and shirt and eased himself into the water to retrieve the stones before someone cut their foot. As Margo watched the reconnaissance operation from the grass, she noticed a series of small round scars on Lou's right side, situated between his arm pit and waist. They were about one inch apart and formed two parallel lines. They looked like cigarette burns or chicken pox scars that had become infected before healing. But it was the symmetry of their positioning that caught her attention. Seeing them made her wonder what had happened to him. When he got out of the pool he yelled to Angela, "bring me my shirt," and as he put it on, she got the feeling he was anxious to cover up what had been exposed. It would be almost half a century later when Margo learned their origin.

LATER, CAJOLED FROM THE SWIMMING POOL, THE KIDS SETTLED on the grass with hotdogs and lemonade. Clustered under an umbrella, their parents finally relaxed after taking turns being lifeguard. Lou had just finished what in the archives of favorite stories became known as the "telephone bill story." As head chemist for a major soft drink company, he was one of two people who carried in his head the much-guarded formula for Pronto, the bottled drink that was sold all over the world. He'd been in Hong Kong for over two weeks, opening a new plant and called home from his hotel room to give Angela the flight information for his return. "Carl picked up the phone," Lou said, "I could tell he was not as impressed by the sound of my voice as he was by the cartoons blasting on the tv in the background. I told him to get Mommy. He mumbled 'Okay,' put the receiver down on the table and forgot the part about getting Mommy."

They were all laughing over the way Carl dissed his executive father and the huge phone bill that resulted, when suddenly, Lou got serious and said, "All this travelling is finally going to stop. "I'm changing jobs and we're moving to New Jersey!"

Angela put down the empty ice bucket she had just collected for a refill trip to the kitchen. She looked at Margo and smiled a wide joyous smile, confirming their secret, before sitting on the arm of Lou's chair.

"What? Where did that come from," Kevin asked in astonishment. Margo squealed, "We'll be geographically closer again?"

"Yes and no. We're buying a house in Princeton. We're still going to be about seventy miles apart, but at least we'll be in the same state. No more bridges to cross or tunnels to crawl through in the car."

"Tell us. I'm so excited for you."

"The house is brand new. No more rebuilding this money pit of broken pipes and rotting wood," Lou said, as he extended his arms to gesture towards the house, where a ladder leaned precariously against a loose gutter.

Within the next fifteen minutes, Margo and Kevin learned of the months of planning that preceded their announcement. Lou was leaving the beverage field for pharmaceuticals. He would be overseeing the rollout of a new medicine at one of the major drug companies in south Jersey.

"The schools are supposed to be the best in the state, and that's a major factor in where we are going. South Jersey is poised to be the pharmaceutical corridor of the tri-state area. It's a dream now, but if I ever open my own business that's where I'd like to be."

With the announcement came the back story. Lou's job had gone sour. Now that the situation was resolved and relegated to the past, they learned how miserable he had been. "Going in each day was making me sick," Lou confided.

Angela had never said a word to Margo.

After the fireworks dwindled, and the kids were loaded into the car, once again the four friends vowed, "Every Fourth of July, just like today. We'll spend it together, no matter where we live."

With that promise in mind, Kevin and Margo pulled away from the curb in their old boat of a Buick.

AFTER ANGELA AND LOU MOVED, HOWEVER, IT WAS MOSTLY Margo and Kevin who corralled their kids into the car and drove the seventy miles to Princeton to spend a day together. Angela, unlike Margo, loved to busy herself behind her huge Viking stove, stirring simmering pots of sauce for dinner, happy to be feeding all of them.

"Why don't you come to us for the day?" Margo asked more than once.

Angela would hesitate, "Let me ask Lou and call you back."

There was often an excuse. "Lou works so hard. He doesn't like to leave home on the weekends. Lou is travelling next week. Lou has a cold." Or they would make a date and at the last-minute cancel. Margo sometimes wondered if Angela was deferring to Lou, if she might enjoy getting away for a day. But it was their marriage and who was she to question it?

As the children morphed into teen-agers, it became more and more difficult to coordinate a visit. They had to contend with school schedules, soccer practice, football practice, base-ball practice, Cub Scouts, Girl Scouts, birthday parties, home-work, and more homework. It all took precedence, but every so often, the stars aligned, and they pulled it off.

WINTER OF 1979 WAS THEIR LAST VISIT WITH ALL THE KIDS TO Lou and Angela's home in Princeton. After they pulled up in the overcrowded station wagon, amidst the commotion of sorting through ice skates and hockey sticks for the game that would take place on the frozen pond behind their house, Angela whispered, "We've got some good news to tell you." She was as excited as Margo had ever seen her.

Margo stopped short of unloading hockey sticks and helmets. Wide-eyed, she looked at Angela and mouthed "Pregnant?"

"Oh God, no," Angela laughed. "It's Lou's news, we'll tell you later."

After the ice hockey game, Margo chopped vegetables for the salad and Kevin spread garlic paste on the four loaves of Italian bread soon to be devoured by the gang of teen-agers in the family room who claimed to be starving. Angela stirred the sauce and Lou fidgeted with some new gadget to open the wine, when Margo couldn't wait any longer and asked, "So, what's your news?"

Lou stopped fidgeting, "I'm finally doing it. Starting my own operation. I've rented a warehouse that includes office space, and I'm in the process of getting the equipment I need to produce sucrose sugar spheres. I will become a supplier for Atkinson & Allen. My first customer."

"Whoa, how did you manage to snag them as your first customer?" Kevin asked, knowing from his own business experience just how hard it was to land a major corporation.

Lou explained, "My experience as a chemist at Pronto made me an expert with sugar. The pharmaceutical business uses sucrose-based spheres which are then coated with the active ingredients in a particular drug. These coated spheres are what you see in a typical time-release capsule. The spheres must be made with precision because the surface area determines the dosage of the drug. I've developed a way of making the spheres with more precision, which is critical to the drug companies."

"I've been reading about the recent boom in generic drugs," Kevin said.

"Yes, and South Jersey is already a hub of the global pharmaceutical industry."

"So, you will be manufacturing the sugar spheres and selling them to the pharma companies?"

"That's the hope," Lou said, as he knocked on the wood of the old oak kitchen table that Angela had found and refinished years ago.

Angela chimed in, "I'll work in the office, answering phones, taking care of the clerical end of things."

"I know a family business has been your dream since the boys were little," Kevin said. "Have you decided on a name yet?

"Take a guess," Lou said.

Kevin was quick to respond, "Romano's." Margo agreed. "The family name for the family business?"

"We thought of that. But—what do you think of PARC Labs?"

Margo got it immediately. It took a minute for Kevin to latch on to their long-standing acronym for the boys, Paulo, Arturo, Roberto, and Carlo—PARC. "I love it," she said.

"You are already primed for transitioning the boys into the business," Kevin added.

Margo could tell by the grin on Lou's face that he loved the observation, loved that they both got the significance of PARC Labs. "It's been the dream. I'll give them jobs after college and let them learn the ropes. I hope at least one of them will study chemistry, like I did. Maybe one of them marketing, and another, finance."

"It would be such fun having them all working with us," Angela added.

"Paul's majoring in history now and I'm trying to steer him

towards law school, which would certainly be an asset to the company as we grow."

"Are any of them interested in chemistry?"

"Maybe Carl. He's still in high school, so who knows," Lou said.

Angela shook her head and said good-naturedly, "Unless they put chemistry in the architecture department, I don't see him following in his father's footsteps. He likes to build things."

"Well, I want him to build our business. Same thing," Lou said with a grin.

"Yeah, same thing," Angela said with a conciliatory shrug. "We'll see."

"Maybe someday, but for now it's just me and Angela," Lou said. Giving up on the gadget for a simple corkscrew, he poured wine for the four of them. They clinked glasses in a toast to acknowledge the humble beginnings of the company, from which Angela and Lou's lives would evolve like some version of an Italian Opera.

THAT SAME AFTERNOON, AFTER DINNER, WHILE THE TEENS PLAYED boisterous monopoly in the family room, Margo loaded the dishwasher, and Angela scooped ice cream onto warm wedges of pie. Lou and Kevin packed up the station wagon for the trip home. Ice skates, hockey sticks, helmets, kneepads, elbow pads and wet gloves were all accounted for. Content, after Angela's lasagna and the warmth of the kitchen, Kevin later described to Margo how they'd stood in their shirt sleeves breathing the cold air. As he stuffed the last helmet into the back of the wagon, Lou looked at him with that conspiratorial gleam in his eyes and said, "Do you have room for one more client in that company of yours, Kevin?"

It had been a few years earlier when Kevin left his job to form his own accounting company, Kevin Conroy, Ltd. Lou knew how hard Kevin was working to garner clients and build the business. The ease with which he offered PARC Labs as a new client wasn't lost on Kevin. Caught unawares, he blurted, "Are you kidding, Lou. Of course, I have room. I'm honored to be asked. This will go down as the easiest sale I'll ever have the pleasure of making. It's a gift."

"That's what friends are for," Lou said, pleased with himself. "I know we are a small company as we get started, but I think we are going to grow fast, especially when the boys come on board after college. Hopefully PARC Labs will become one of your biggest clients."

The offer, the gift, so casually rendered in the Princeton driveway, was something Kevin never forgot.

IN THE YEARS THAT FOLLOWED, MARGO OFTEN WONDERED, as she reached for a capsule for a headache or sore knee, if the ingredients had begun their long journey to their medicine cabinet from the PARC plant.

Once again, proximity and circumstances prompted them to map a new geography to accommodate their changing lives. It would serve them for almost two decades.

Once every two months Kevin and Margo met at Bella Napoli, a little Italian restaurant in Hillsdale, a town midway between them, to catch-up as they reported on their lives and the kids' mishaps and successes. Nothing was off limits for turning into a laugh. They had a backlog of stories to come back to, and back to, to entertain each other. There was Kevin's running out of gas in the Lincoln Tunnel while Margo was seven months pregnant, Lou's five-hundred-dollar phone call from Hong Kong, Margo's mortification at dumping a bowl of popcorn over a prestigious speaker right before she was to introduce him to the audience, and of course their shared history in the blizzard of '59, and the "be nice" prelate soon after. Lou especially had a way of pushing the boundaries with language, which, combined with his infectious laughter made the untoward incidents hysterical and turned their little tragedies into comedy.

They entertained each other. They had a good time. No one was willing to spoil it with a problem or a grief. The list of things they didn't share grew.

Chapter Six

1980s

During the early eighties, while Angela and Lou's lives were flourishing, Margo and Kevin's crashed. A few years after Lou established PARC Labs, Kevin went into partnership with Will Wilkins, a man several years his senior. Together, they established an accounting firm, Wilkins & Conroy. They had office space at a prestigious Fifth Avenue address in Manhattan. It was the era of business lunches and expense accounts. Celebratory drinks at one of the cocktail lounges that sprung up like mushrooms along the city streets, were a common and accepted business practice. As Wilkins & Conroy garnered more accounts, the reasons to celebrate multiplied. As the business grew, so did Kevin's drinking.

In 1980, Kevin's partner, Will, lost a court battle over alimony and child support in a contentious divorce. He creatively took care of his newly mandated obligations to his ex-wife and two sons by simply disappearing. One day he was in the office, the next gone without a trace. His family and the business were left in financial disarray. Initially, Kevin expected Will would, if not spontaneously show up as unexpectedly as he had disappeared, at least communicate. It wasn't until five years later, the day before Kevin was scheduled to act on a court order Will's ex-wife had obtained, that Will returned. Kevin was prepared to meet with attorneys and sign over Will's half of the business, which had been put in escrow, to the ex-wife, who had no idea of Will's whereabouts either.

During those years, Kevin's deal-making lunches with Will turned into lonely hours of drinking alone, as he coped with the loss of his partner and friend. The drinking started slowly. In the early days as the kids and Margo sat down for dinner, one of them would ask, "Where's dad?"

"Working late," She'd answer, as she slipped a plate of food in the oven for when he arrived. As the months went by, his arrival time became more and more unpredictable. The kids just stopped asking and counted on seeing him the following morning.

Kevin had more than once refuted Margo's accusations comparing him to his father, who had been a binge drinker. For as long as she knew him, Kevin had quietly carried the shame and anger his father engendered in him ever since he became aware of the alcoholism as a child. "I will never be like my father," he would retort angrily when Margo mistakenly thought reminding him of his father would make him stop drinking. It was hard for her to understand how he didn't see what was happening. She could remember his hurt the day he graduated from college. The youngest and only of his mother's three sons to finish their degrees, Kevin walked up the aisle to receive his Bachelor of Science diploma. His proud mother, his two older brothers and Margo applauded wildly, while his father, barely conscious, drunk on cheap wine, stole the day with his absence. They were getting married the following Saturday and Kevin and his brothers spent the week hiding bottles of alcohol and monitoring their father to get him sober enough to attend the wedding.

Margo's life had turned into Kevin's mother's life. She covered it up with everyone, even Angela and Lou. When they got together, she didn't share that they were in debt, that she feared the business would not survive and there would be no money for college tuitions. She didn't know if her marriage would survive. Like Kevin's mother, she pretended otherwise. In retrospect Margo wondered if this holding back said something about their friendship, diminished it? Or did it say more about the times they lived in when the veneer of happiness had to be polished and maintained?

Throughout those chaotic years, Margo joined Alanon, an anonymous support group for the families of alcoholics. She sent the reluctant children to a six-week series of Alateen meetings designed to educate and help kids cope with the unpredictability of living with an alcoholic. Each Thursday evening, as the time to leave for the meeting drew near, there were angry outbursts. "Why do we have to go? I'm not going. It's stupid." They slammed through the back hall, gathering their jackets, banging doors for emphasis. "Why are you making us do this?"

She never told them her secondary agenda. She had watched Kevin disavow his father's drinking from the time she met him in high school, yet he failed to recognize the symptoms when they overtook him. Alcoholism had a genetic component; the children were vulnerable, and she wanted them to know that before it was too late.

Still bellowing protests, they hurled themselves into the car, Declan and Maura arguing about who would drive and Finn climbing into the back seat with a book tucked under his arm. Although they left like lions they returned like lambs. Subdued, no longer angry, they each went to their rooms. Some intangible moments of calm seemed to have touched them. Margo let them be. They had received something at the meeting. She didn't have to know what it was.

Years later, she asked each of them what the most significant thing was they had learned at Alateen. The answer: "It was not my fault." Never would she have dreamed at the time that each had blamed themselves for their father's addiction to alcohol.

During those most difficult years, Margo and Kevin rarely saw Angela and Lou. Life was so unpredictable; they were not getting together with any of their friends. There were sporadic phone calls with Angela, during which Margo shared everything but the most important aspect of their lives, Kevin's drinking. She resumed therapy with the psychologist who had shepherded her as she fought her way out of depression years earlier. She continued with college. These two strands of her experience knit themselves into a lifesaving goal. After attaining her undergraduate degree in the late seventies, she enrolled in a master's program in psychology, not unlike many *wounded healers* who embraced psychology to help others after experiencing healing themselves. She needed to prepare herself for a career. She needed to earn money. She didn't think her marriage was going to survive.

In 1983, Kevin entered rehab for alcohol treatment. It was during the long weeks of the treatment program that Margo learned Kevin had gone to Lou months earlier and borrowed ten-thousand dollars. Angela had known and never said a word to Margo, never asked a question or embarrassed her.

Margo doubted Lou realized Kevin was drinking when he loaned him the money; nevertheless, it was a generous act. When Kevin entered treatment, the pretending ended. Before being discharged, as part of the ten-step program, Kevin committed to call Lou and level with him about his drinking, his lying, and how it impacted the business and the money he had borrowed. It wasn't an easy call to make.

The day following his discharge, Kevin, trailed by the dog who sensed his unease, prepared to call Lou. Margo knew he hadn't slept the previous night. She heard him padding around at three in the morning, organizing the files from the New York office, from which he had been evicted.

Before closing the door to his hastily created home office, he asked Margo not to listen to his end of the conversation. A familiar anxiety arose in her chest. On the one hand, she understood. It was enough for him to anticipate the shame in revealing the truth to Lou without complicating their conversation with how his wife might be judging it. On the other hand, because the previous years had been so full of dishonesty around alcohol, she feared he might not follow through and make the call at all. Trust had been destroyed. Those early days of recovery were the axis on which the future of the family pivoted.

When Kevin came out of the office an hour later, he told her the call had gone well.

Lou was understanding. He told Kevin he had no idea things were so bad and asked if there was anything he could do to help.

If there was still any lingering doubt about whether Kevin had made the call, it was dispelled a few days later when Margo heard from Angela. She had a sense that Lou asked Angela to call and was sitting at her elbow as they spoke. Angela was lighthearted and supportive. Yet her message jolted Margo. After a few minutes of small talk, she said, "Lou needs the money that he loaned Kevin."

Hearing this, humiliation and panic coursed through her body as she quickly calculated when she could scrape the money together. She promised to send a check in three weeks, anticipating that would give her enough time to collect funds owed to the business, funds Kevin had let slip while he was drinking. When she hung up the phone, she immediately wrote a check for ten-thousand dollars and placed it in the center of her desk. It remained there like a timebomb, as she counted the days until the three weeks went by and she would sign and send it.

As the day approached, Angela called again. "Just a reminder."

Flummoxed, assuring Angela, "yes, yes, I know," she scooped up the check, quickly addressed an envelope and sent it. Two days later she got a call from Angela. She was laughing, "We got the check Margo, but it wasn't signed."

Margo was once again humiliated. But more than that, it was Angela's trademark laugh that cut like a knife. Perhaps the laugh was an indication of her nervousness about making the call. Perhaps she didn't know what to say without getting too personal, since Margo had not confided in her during those years when everything was falling apart. Or perhaps it was one of those hilarious stories they would tell and tell again.

It would be many months before she could face them again. Once again, Lou recast the unsigned check into comedy borne out of what to her had been a tragedy. He turned it into a Lucille Ball moment, and they all knew, "Everyone loves Lucy."

The incident of the check was reduced to a blip in their relationship. If Lou ever felt taken advantage of for believing whatever story Kevin told him when he asked for the loan, he never brought it up. Margo told herself Lou's silence was a testimony to friendship, an indication that there remained for all of them that pull to return to the place where it had all begun, the way spawning salmon fight river currents, swimming upstream to return to the source.

As Margo and Kevin's lives got back on track, they resumed their halfway dinners every few months. By then, Bella Napoli was long gone. Walmart found the location as amenable to access shoppers as they had to meet for dinner. A group of neighborhood stores, including Bella Napoli, that had thrived there for twenty years, was replaced by the big box store and an equally huge parking lot as urban sprawl ate into the fields and meadows of south Jersey. Mario, the owner, and most of his staff, relocated to Lunello about ten miles west. They followed. No longer halfway between them, the extra ten miles for Margo and Kevin were just absorbed into the destination to accommodate their new geography.

By 1987, Margo was completing the requirements for her master's degree. Kevin wanted to surprise her with a party. He called Lou and told him, "I want it to be a roast where everyone brings a funny memory to share. I need a Master of Ceremonies and since you're the funniest person I know, will you MC?"

"Sure," Lou said enthusiastically, "I'd be honored. I already know what story I'm going to tell during the roast."

Kevin gave Lou a few alternate dates, in essence picking the date around Lou's sure availability. They discussed how to pull off the surprise. Since both of their wedding anniversaries were in June, they came up with a diversion plan. Kevin casually mentioned to Margo that he had made a date with Lou and Angela for a Saturday night in June to celebrate both their anniversaries.

The night of the party, family and friends emerged from the shadows of a darkened restaurant and shouted their congratulations. It took a few minutes for Margo to comprehend the banner draped across the room "Congratulations on your MASTER'S," and realize this was not an anniversary dinner with Angela and Lou. Overwhelmed, it was a while before she settled in. After greeting friends, she had not seen in years, counting the blessings of family and friends, some who had travelled from out of state, she realized someone was missing. "Are Angela and Lou here?" she asked Kevin.

"Not now. I'll tell you tomorrow," he whispered myste-riously.

"Are they okay?"

"Yes. Don't worry. They're fine. It's a long story."

The next day Kevin revealed that Angela called three hours before the party to say Lou was fighting a cold.

"I thought I could convince him to change his mind. I was depending on him to MC the roast."

Angela put Lou on the phone, but the answer was the same, "I'm jet lagged and just not up to a long drive." Kevin scram-bled among the guests and another friend took over as MC. The evening was salvaged.

A few days later, a handwritten note arrived "from the desk of Lou Romano." It read, "Angela and I are both terribly disappointed we couldn't participate in your master's degree party. Now that you take your place in history next to great women like Joan of Arc, Mother Theresa, Margaret Thatcher, and Edith Bunker, we can all take pride in knowing you. Just one question. Did you really think it was an anniversary dinner all along? Or did you figure it out eventually?" Once again Lou's charming note disarmed her.

A few weeks later they met for dinner at Lunello. As they approached the table, there was Lou, healthy as ever ...

He began the evening by ordering champagne while Kevin ordered seltzer. "Let's toast Margo on that master's degree," *No, how was the party? Sorry we weren't there. Who did you get to MC?* Letting Kevin down at the last minute had no place at the table. There was never any further explanation about why they hadn't shown up, and neither Lou nor Angela ever brought it up again. The occasion passed into history.

The fact that they never discussed it may have bothered Margo more than their cancelling. The evening had been important to her, and she wanted to talk about it when they met for dinner, relay some of the stories told during the roast, talk about their friends who were there, many of whom Angela and Lou knew. She wanted to hear that Lou's cold turned into a flu that lasted a week, something serious enough to ameliorate the disappointment for their not coming. On the drive home Margo commented on the avoided conversation. Kevin gave a sigh and said, "I know. But I suspect there have been times we disappointed them too."

"I guess," she said. A long-suppressed guilt filled her as she thought about Kevin's delight when he was asked to be Arturo's godfather. In the Italian tradition, a sustaining role was carved out within the family for the godfather. He was expected to play a significant part in the life of the child on holidays, birthdays, and each time the child received one of the Catholic sacraments.

For the Conroy's with their Irish traditions, the role of godparent as a special surrogate the day of the baptism, gradually lost its shine. It was not binding by any law within the church or state. As time went on, if one of the children came home from religious education class where the topic came up and asked, "Who's my godfather?" Margo would search her brain. She could never keep straight which of Kevin's or her brothers or sisters was godparent for which of the children. They all melded together in her mind, the same way she might forget who the second-grade teacher was for each of them. It didn't really matter if they all got through second grade.

During the difficult years, Margo and Kevin often failed to send a Christmas present or remember Artie's birthday. They missed his confirmation because the day was taken up with Maura's piano recital. Neither Angela nor Lou ever brought it up, never faulted them. Yet, as she counted the arrows in her quiver of resentments, she couldn't help but wonder if they thought they'd made a mistake asking Kevin to be Artie's godfather.

THEIR RELATIONSHIP DEEPENED IN A MOST EXTRAORDINARY WAY in the early nineties. During dinner at Lunello, Lou surprised them with "the kids are all out of the house, we're still young, let's take a trip to Europe together."

"Really. You mean it?"

"Let's go to Paris," Lou suggested enthusiastically.

"That's the one place in Europe we've been," Kevin said. "We visited Declan there a couple of years ago when he was studying in Arles."

"But it's such a great city," Lou lobbied. "I've always dreamed of showing it to Angela. We've got a lot of years ahead of us to travel. Let's start with Paris."

They knew Lou had travelled all over the world during his early career. But Angela had never been out of the county. Now that they were ready to travel, Margo and Kevin accommodated. Being with their friends on vacation was more important than the city they visited. Lou stepped into the role of primary planner and tour guide. He knew a bit of French and his flawless memory made him a fountain of information. It was to be a leisurely trip with no predetermined tours, just four friends exploring Paris together. One thing Margo remembers vividly was how Angela and Lou held hands as they walked every avenue and boulevard of the city. Kevin and she tended to lose each other pretty frequently as they wandered off to pursue their own interests; Angela and Lou still reached for each other like newlyweds.

After they arrived, realizing Lourdes was a few hours train ride south of Paris, Margo asked, "How would you like to take an overnight trip to visit the shrine?"

"Yes, let's do it. I had no idea we would be so close," Angela said with enthusiasm.

Lou remained silent. Angela pressed, "You've never been to Lourdes, have you Lou? I've always wanted to see it."

"We'll see," he said.

Over the next few days, they would reconsider Lourdes. Disappointment registered on Angela's face, then hope, as they all heard another "We'll see," from Lou, followed by his insisting how easy it would be to pick up railroad tickets at the last minute.

In the end, Kevin and Margo went to Lourdes and Angela and Lou remained in Paris. When they returned thirty-six hours later, Angela was interested in every detail of their excursion. "Tell us about the miracles. Do they really take place?" she asked.

Margo told them about the awe-inspiring outdoor Mass, where thousands of people, from just about every country on earth, prayed the same prayers, in their respective languages like one international community. Kevin described the hundreds of crutches abandoned on the wall by the "cured;" of young mothers filling their babies' bottles with the healing waters, then sitting on the stone walls of the grotto as their babies gulped the water. They recounted seeing hundreds of children dressed in white, sitting in wheelchairs decorated with roses as they received their first communion, the thousands of candles burning night and day. Angela's eyes filled with tears as she soaked up the stories. Lou did not engage but kept his eyes on a paper napkin where he was busy translating pithy remarks printed in French.

During that trip they toured the Louvre. Angela and Margo were standing together, their shoulders almost touching, gazing at a Monet painting. Angela loved the painting and told Margo it brought back a vivid memory of her sixteenth summer. Her father had rented a cabin in the Poconos so the family could get away from the boiling streets of Brooklyn. While there, she became friends with a group of teens and one morning six of them piled into someone's father's pick-up truck in search of an abandoned quarry. Local lore claimed the water that filled the quarry pit was so deep, it was thought bottomless. With a faraway look in her eyes, she described how after parking the pick-up on a deserted dirt road, the little band ascended the steep slope. Her eyes still glued to the painting that was captivating her, she said, "Coming upon the quarry at the top of the wooded trail was all white light and blue sky. It had been mined for limestone and the white walls of the hollowed-out pit were filled with water from rain and snow and springs that coursed through the rocks. It was the clearest blue I'd ever seen. There were no fish, no lily pads, no muddy banks, or sandy beach. It was like looking into a pool of sky." With growing excitement, she described how there was no shallow end to this pit. You entered only one way. A jump or dive from one of the jiggered outcroppings of limestone into the bottomless deep. Dares of who's going to jump first echoed across the mountain. "I was so scared." She paused as she remembered.

"Did you jump?" Margo asked.

"I did. I plunged into that cold blue pit of sky," she said proudly as she adjusted the strap on her handbag and prepared to move on to the next painting. Her reverie broken, she leaned towards Margo and said, "sometimes I wonder what happened to that brave girl."

Many years later, well after tragedy had struck, when she said wistfully, "I never did get to Lourdes," Margo thought of that girl, the one who had plunged into the deep blue of the quarry.

Chapter Seven

1997

Lou placed a clear plastic bag on the table at Lunello with a flourish. Margo and Kevin had arrived a few minutes earlier and Margo could see through the plastic that it contained a book.

"Give this to Finn," Lou said. "He mentioned he's read all of Graham Greene except this one, *The Heart of the Matter*. I told him, being a Graham Greene fan myself, I happen to have it in my library."

Both Margo and Kevin were flummoxed. Surprised. "You've been talking to Finn?"

"Yes, several times. Didn't he mention it? I called him shortly after our last dinner. I'll tell you; your son is direct, and I like that. He got right to the point."

"Why me?" Finn asked.

Lou didn't hesitate with his response. "It's the family connection. We go so far back. I still remember following you around the backyard while you were in diapers and scooping you up as you tried to crawl under a fence. That history means so much to me. I feel I really know who I'd be getting, especially bringing someone in over my sons. It could be a perfect match and an opportunity for all of us to make a lot of money and have fun while we're doing it."

Margo imagined Finn chuckling. Who else but Lou would use the word fun in a recruiting call? Who else would remember him in diapers?

Lou told Finn he liked to keep things simple. Unless there was an emergency at the plant, weekends would be his own. Travel was local. Lou knew from Kevin that Finn's life had been shuttling all over the globe for the past seven or eight years.

"That got his attention," Lou said, "We've been talking for the last several weeks."

Margo was surprised but pleased. She knew Finn wouldn't waste Lou's time if he still wasn't interested. It was exciting to learn that talks had been going on.

"Since getting reacquainted with your son, I'm more excited than ever about bringing him on. But I did have to correct him on one thing, no more Mr. Romano. From now on call me Lou."

How like Finn, Margo thought, to retain the respectful "Mr." from his childhood, even as he confronted Lou with his doubts about his offer.

"So, I understand you've never read Graham Green's *Heart of the Matter*," Margo said to Finn when she called him the following week.

"Whaat? Where did that come from?"

"I have a copy of it for you, a gift from Lou Romano."

"Ahh, you saw him, and he told you we've been talking?"

"Yes, you never mentioned anything!"

"Nothing to mention really. We're just talking."

Nothing to mention! That's the difference between sons

and daughters, Margo thought. If this had been Maura, they would have had long thoughtful conversations every step of the way.

"Are you seriously considering it?"

"I'm listening. It's a solid business. Lou sent me his financials a few weeks ago and I've done my own analysis. There is great potential for growth and maybe eventually taking it public."

"But? I sense there's still a 'but.'"

"Well, the fact that it is a family business. I'm still very, very wary. There's so much that could go wrong. But the thought of a less fraught lifestyle in the suburbs, a home surrounded by grass and trees, maybe a dog. That's enticing. Audrey and I have been talking about that."

"Did you tell him about your concerns about the family business?"

"Yes, during our initial conversation, and each time we talk. He downplays it. He claims PARC Labs is a business, like any other. He is the sole proprietor and while three of his sons work there, none of them has the experience or aspirations to run it. They are all making a nice living and have their niche contributing to the company. He claims they have had many discussions about bringing in someone before he started interviewing candidates several months ago."

"Do you trust him on that explanation?"

"I believe he believes it. But so many pitfalls can emerge from bringing in someone from outside the family. Boundaries get blurred and business communications can get bogged down in family drama, sibling rivalry, feelings of inferiority, jealousy, middle-child syndrome, father issues, mother issues, power, money, guilt. The list grows."

"But none of that is going on in the Romano family."

"Not now, but there's no guarantee about what the future will bring. Things can change. I need to meet with his sons and get a sense of how each of them feels about their father's long-term plan before I do anything."

A FEW WEEKS LATER, ON A SUNNY SATURDAY MORNING, FINN drove from Manhattan, through the Lincoln Tunnel, down the NJ Turnpike and on to the bucolic roads of Princeton to visit PARC Lab's facilities. Lou was waiting for him in the empty parking lot that surrounded the office complex and warehouse. "I hardly recognized him," Finn told his parents. "He's gained a lot of weight since I last saw him at my wedding, and I had to smile as I watched him make a show of extricating his large body from his BMW convertible."

Lou took him on a tour of the offices and the plant where the big stainless-steel drums that synthesized the pharmaceutical spheres gleamed in the Sunday quiet. He unlocked the backdoor to a loading dock where the raw materials were delivered, and the finished products loaded in huge containers and trucked to the pharmaceutical companies.

Finn was impressed by all he learned about the company. Afterwards they went to a local diner for lunch. "I started to feel the balance shift on my readiness to work with Lou. I could feel myself getting excited about the business. I think I can develop it, give him what he wants. But I still want to meet with Artie, Rob, and Carl, both individually and as a group to make my own judgement."

"Did you mention that to Lou?" Kevin asked.

"Yes, he's all for it. He just laughed and said, 'Be my guest. You'll find they are all happy with their positions, but none of them have the vision or ambition to guide us into the future. I've discussed it with all of them and they are all on board.'"

Lou told Finn he envisioned bringing him on board as VP of Strategic Planning. That would give Finn the opportunity to get an overview of every aspect of the business. Beyond strategic planning, he saw him gradually rotating through manufacturing, finance, sales, development, human resources—all the departments. As Finn gained more familiarity and expertise within each area, Lou envisioned a gradual shift of leadership. Within two years, the various departments would start reporting to Finn directly, as Lou removed himself from the day-to-day operations.

"That's when I'm going to call the piano teacher and start to take lessons, and maybe even buy an apartment in Manhattan for getaway weekends."

OVER THE NEXT FEW WEEKS, FINN SET UP MEETINGS WITH Artie, Rob, and Carl, individually and as a group. As Lou predicted, they were all enthusiastic, especially Artie. Finn became more and more convinced that Lou had read his sons correctly; no one was harboring any resentments or sense of having been passed over by an interloper. They welcomed the challenge of growing the business. He genuinely liked the three men the ice hockey playing teen-agers had become. He could envision working with them. "I've gone from disinterest to mild interest to seriously considering taking the job," he told Margo and Kevin.

A business plan started to take shape in Finn's head even before he committed to join. However, the "Perils of Working for a Family Business," remained with him like a red flag on a racetrack. He discussed it with Audrey. At business school, she had read the same case studies as Finn, of family business's floundering when the founder stepped aside. More failed than succeeded. It was a risk. They came up with a plan to reach out to a group of six of his friends who were former class-mates at Stanford. They had become close over the course of their degrees and relied on each other for support when making career decisions. One by one, Finn called his friends and discussed his business opportunity and his concerns with them.

The Stanford reunion was scheduled for a few months later. When the group gathered, with cold beers and peanuts on the patio of the house they had rented for the long weekend, Finn announced he was near to making the decision to accept Lou's offer. They were supportive but realistic. Their main concerns were the family business aspect of the commitment.

They reminded him of the stories of corporate sabotage and the challenge of making significant changes as an outsider, how family members, especially when working closely with the heir apparent, can grow to resent the newcomer for legitimate or made-up reasons. A second caution, scarier to Finn, was how common it was for founders of companies to change their minds as the time to give up control of their creation became a reality. They asked Finn his gut feelings about Lou, and if there was any sign of him being less than resolute.

He told them he believed Lou was fully invested in the plan and that Lou believed it was going to work. His biggest question was, "do I avoid the risk on the chance that something changes in the future." They pointed out that there would be clues along the way as he assumed more and more of the decision making, that a change of heart wouldn't happen in a vacuum.

To confront these concerns, one of his friends suggested Finn find a seminar that openly addressed those very topics and ask Lou to attend with him.

Finn liked the idea. It would mean having professional third parties present to set the agenda and provide the opportunity for both Lou and him to consider and discuss the situation from each other's perspective. Finn's only hesitation was he didn't want to insult Lou.

"It won't be insulting Finn," his friends encouraged, "just part of your due diligence. This is the last piece, the only stum-

bling block. It's worth a try. If he objects that tells you something too."

The seminar Finn found at Columbia University promised
open group discussion, in real time, of the actual business situations facing the participants who had signed up for the seminar.
Geared towards both the entrepreneurs and the candidates
being groomed for positions in family-owned businesses, it was
organized around the potential risks for both parties.

Lou could barely contain, not only his surprise, but the
coffee that flew from his mouth, as he listened to Finn's request
that he attend a postgraduate seminar at Columbia University
with him. "Really, what next, a field trip to Great Adventure?"

But he went. Enthusiastically. For six consecutive weeks, he
brought his sense of humor with him and everyone in the
seminar loved him for the intelligence laced with wit that he
brought to the table. Finn had to laugh himself when Lou
announced to the group of about sixteen participants, "I've
built a multi-million-dollar business and who, but this fellow
could get me back in school, paying his tuition no less." They
were enjoying each other, and they were enjoying the seminar.

Reassured that he had done his homework, eight months
after that first meeting in the parking lot, Finn signed a contract
and joined PARC Labs Corp as Vice President of Strategic
Planning. It was January of 1997. He was thirty-three years
old. He and Audrey packed up their tiny New York apartment
for the old farmhouse they purchased in Cranbury, a small
country town outside Princeton. Surrounded by wide-open
fields, where cows manicured the grasses, they picked wild-
flowers growing along the road as they walked their golden
retriever puppy. So different from the steel canyons of New
York City and the fourteen-to-sixteen-hour workdays they left
behind.

THREE MONTHS LATER, DURING DINNER AT LUNELLO, LOU entertained them by describing Finn's move into headquarters. Lou had reshuffled his son's offices and created a large office for Finn adjacent to his own office so they would have easy access to each other as Finn assumed more and more responsibility. Standing up between tables in the crowded restaurant, he imitated Finn, juggling a lopsided cardboard box overflowing with "tombstones," the same ones he had stored and retrieved from his old attic bedroom, engraved with his name and the name of companies he was instrumental in helping. There was a photo of Audrey and another of their golden retriever destined for a prominent place in his shiny new office. This was followed by Lou's hilarious characterization of Finn maneuvering an "enormous painting of the New York skyline" through his office door, turning it every which way to angle it around corners, bumping his head on the wall in the process. Lou's affectionate portrayal of Finn's bumbling attempt to move the picture had them in stitches, but, more than that, Margo realized he was truly talking about Finn in much the same way he described Artie's short lived Las Vegas marriage or Carl's shoes from Barneys. He was treating him like a son.

It was soon after, seeing the painting of New York still on the floor, leaning against a wall, that Lou teased Finn, "Are you staying, or is that painting on the floor a sign that you're temporary?"

Finn hung it on the wall opposite his desk that very day. He was there to stay.

Chapter Eight

1998

"Take a look at this," Lou said one Saturday night a year later, as he proudly placed a slick multicolored brochure on the white tablecloth at Lunello. It was a gorgeous, mouthwatering display of confections and toppings for baking, the new specialty food product line his company had developed. The graphics were of an artist's palette brimming with an inviting array of pink, green, yellow, and violet confections. A paintbrush was superimposed at its perimeter, inviting the customer to be an artist with this new brand of toppings.

"See what your son has us into now? I just picked these up from the printer."

"He's not kidding, we literally stopped and picked them up on our way here so he could show you," Angela said.

"What do you think? I'm so proud," Lou said, pointing to the brand name, Bakers Palette, printed in a flowing black script across the top of the brochure.

"We took sugar ingredients that we already work with for the pharmaceutical industry and developed this whole new brand. Finn hired a freelance artist who worked on the design and logo. He applied for the trademark, and it came through. Now we're launching Bakers Palette within the baking industry. We have already put it in production."

Finn hadn't said a word to them about the details of what he was working on, which wasn't unusual. They knew he was happy at PARC Labs and that's what mattered. The actual work projects were secondary, as they were with all their children. Once again, they were excited to share Lou and Angela's enthusiasm, and before the evening was over, picked up their glasses as Lou proposed a toast, "Here's to the skinny little glass of milk. He's got us shining like a star! One of the best decisions I ever made."

It had been the right decision for Finn too. He and Audrey were happy living in the bucolic countryside, away from the noise and traffic of New York City. Their weeks began to hum to the rhythms of crickets chirping and mourning doves cooing. The little farmhouse built in the early nineteen hundreds became their avocation, the outlet for their creative instincts.

Finn discovered a love of woodworking and bought himself a radial arm saw to begin replacing the old woodwork in the dining room. He was teaching himself to measure and miter corners with the same enthusiasm he tackled everything else, enjoying the challenge of installing new oak wainscoting, a chair rail, and ceiling molding.

When Margo and Kevin visited in the spring the kitchen counter was littered with paint chips and swatches of fabric. "Help us pick," Audrey urged. "There are so many choices to make." When Audrey ran to the car to retrieve a display of granite chips for the kitchen countertop, Kevin asked Finn how it was going with Lou and his sons.

"Do you have any more of those family-business concerns?"

"No, not at all," Finn said. "Artie and Rob continue with their responsibilities running the factory, overseeing production, and getting the products delivered to customers. They do it flawlessly, just as Lou predicted. Artie has some really good ideas; I really rely on him. Of the three brothers, I think he probably does have the most potential to eventually run the business. But I've noticed how hard it is for Lou to give him credit."

"How so?"

"He seems unable to trust that the old impulsive behavior of his nineteen-year-old son won't resurface."

"Really? Lou is so generous in so many aspects of his life," Kevin said. "I don't know if you even know this, but during the early eighties, when my business was in trouble, he loaned me ten-thousand dollars to help me through a bad spell."

"I didn't know that. I remember being worried about you and mom at that time, and concerned about my college tuition, but I didn't know he loaned you money. That's good to hear. But he's not generous with praise when it comes to his sons, especially Artie."

Finn explained how Artie had this great idea about doubling up on one of the pieces of equipment they use for pharmaceutical products and making use of it in the confection line. Lou barely took his son seriously. Finn knew Artie was on to something and was eventually able to get through to Lou. "We implemented Artie's idea, and it is saving us a ton of money."

"Did Lou ever acknowledge Artie's role?"

"No. It has somehow morphed into Lou's idea whenever it comes up."

Kevin just shook his head in a quandary, "I don't get it."

"Me either, Lou is so different than you in that respect. You give us all too much credit, even for the small stuff," Finn added.

The three of them knew that to be true. There were times when Margo kicked Kevin under a restaurant table as he bored friends, expanding on one of the children's accomplishments. From the time they were little, anything from catching a fish to winning an award was grist for his pride mill. Each of them was embarrassed if they were present when their father got going, but they knew he was proud of them.

"What about the other boys?" Kevin asked.

"Rob is quiet. He doesn't say a lot but what he does say is always on the mark. He is more of a nine-to-fiver than Artie. He works very hard while he's here, but once he leaves the building for the day, he closes the door behind him and doesn't pay attention again until he returns the next morning. Artie, on the other hand, is always thinking about the next step."

"And Carl?"

"I see less of him than Artie and Rob. He's good at designing space and keeping the physical plant in good shape but I don't interact with him very often. He comes to all the development meetings but really doesn't show much interest in the business end."

"But it might be changing with Carl," Audrey interjected, as she returned with the granite samples and a treat for the dog who had followed her to the car. "Carl invited us over, to see this century-old Victorian house he is restoring by himself."

"Yes," Finn added. "He came alive as he took us around, pointing out where he's replaced rotted beams and exposed a huge fireplace by breaking through a wall. Beautiful work. I saw a different side of him from the grim, shadowy guy I see skulking around the plant."

"Sounds like he doesn't have enough work he likes to do at PARC Labs," Kevin said.

"I think you're right. There isn't enough to keep him busy

or satisfy his need to be creative the way architecture and designing new projects might excite him. But I also think it's hard for him to give up the perks working for his father provides. And it's clear, Lou and Angela want him there."

"I can see where that would be complicated."

"After Carl gave us the construction tour of his house, he offered to give me some advice on fixing up our house. I took him up on it and he came to the lumber yard with me to help me pick out oak planks for the woodwork in the dining room. We had a great day together. He offered to help me install a chair rail and moldings if I get stuck with mitering and measuring. I feel like I'm getting to know him a little more and that feels good."

TWO WEEKS BEFORE CHRISTMAS IN 1998, FINN, HIS CHEEKS red from a trek through the woods, pointed to the enormous fir tree, still tied, and bundled on the sturdy hundred-year-old plank floor in the front room of the house. "We cut it down ourselves this morning on a tree farm not far from here." Margo and Kevin had just arrived to spend a leisurely Sunday decorating the tree with them.

"What a difference from the scraggly trees we used to squeeze into the elevator of our New York apartment," Audrey added, as she removed a pan of cookies from the oven and came to greet them.

After putting the cookies on a trivet to cool, she did a little happy dance with the dog, only too pleased to relinquish his front paws and twirl with her alongside the kitchen table. She sang, "I have an offer for a job in south Jersey. No more long bus commutes into Manhattan."

"That is such good news," Margo said. "I know you've been looking since you left the City."

"Can you tell us who you are negotiating with," Kevin asked, "or is it hush hush until you sign a contract?"

"I can tell you. Confidentially, for now. I'll be the marketing director for a small startup in West Windsor, which is only a few miles from here."

They barely had time to respond when Finn added, "We also found a new fertility doctor who sees no reason why we won't get pregnant."

"Somehow I believe it's going to happen," Audrey said with new confidence. They were both glowing. Although they hadn't discussed it at the time, Margo thought of the pink and blue paint chips that lay amongst the fabric swatches on the kitchen table in the spring.

Later, from his perch on the ladder where he was stringing lights at the top of the tree, Finn said to Kevin, "I plan on talking to Lou after the holidays about expanding my responsibilities at PARC Labs. I've hit all the goals and more that we set in the business plan two years ago."

It was generally Kevin or Margo who initiated a conversation about PARC Labs with their generic questions: How's the job going? Any more worries about being in a family business? Are you still planning to take it public? The usual parent questions, the answers to which they later applied their own formula to evaluate Finn's happiness.

This was different. They could tell Finn was excited. Margo looked at her son on top of the wobbling ladder just as Audrey snatched the dog's collar to slow him down and remove some strands of tinsel attached by static to his snout.

"Could you two have this conversation later, when you're both on the ground?" Margo asked.

"Yes, it can wait Mom."

Later, Audrey unwrapped the last ornament from its tissue paper jacket, a delicate golden globe they had purchased on their honeymoon. Finn returned the empty cartons to a closet.

A fire crackled in the fireplace. Audrey brought out cookies and hot chocolate and Finn lit the tree. Tired, they fell into chairs to enjoy that contented feeling that comes from a Christmas season when everything in life appears to be going right.

"So, finish telling us your story about PARC Labs," Kevin urged.

"A couple of weeks ago, Artie stopped by my office with some really interesting news," Finn began. "He'd been at International Foods on a sales call. He picked up on a rumor from his contact that International Foods was putting together an offer to buy our new business. Seems we've cut into their market shares considerably and they have already lost some major accounts. I think they want to buy it to eliminate us as competitors."

"Is that Bakers Palette?" Margo asked, remembering the brochure Lou had proudly displayed at Lunello.

"Yes, that's it."

"That's amazing. You launched Bakers Palette less than a year ago, right?" Kevin asked.

"Yes. I know there is no way we will ever sell it, but the fact that we have rattled a major competitor speaks for itself. It is validating."

"Could you be tempted to sell if the offer was good enough?"

"No. Not at all. We have established a brand. It's been trademarked. Lou, Artie, Rob, and I have already discussed ways to further build the brand and we have other products in the pipeline that we believe will take off just like the cake toppings. We've developed the plan to grow the company and it's happening even quicker than I anticipated."

"Are you still on course to take PARC Labs public?"

"I'm still working on it as if we are going forward, but, in my opinion, taking the company public would be an adjustment too far, in terms of the way Lou likes to operate."

Kevin smiled knowingly and nodded, understanding Finn's response. But Margo was baffled. "What do you mean?"

"As a privately owned business, Lou can use his own discretion on how to run the company. And he is very good at it. If he wants to spend money on BMWs for family members, put down payments on his son's houses, buy a new warehouse, even give his money away in philanthropic gestures, there's no board or shareholders to prevent it, which is fine, perfectly legal for a private company."

Between Kevin and Finn's tutorial, Margo learned much of the difference between a private and public company has to do with transparency. A public company's shares are traded on a stock exchange, under rigorous scrutiny, while a private company has no such requirements.

Finn went on to explain. "The next step in taking it public is to develop financial statements and disclosures to share with prospective investors. I think with the rapid growth of Bakers Palette and the stability of the pharmaceutical division, the company is strong enough to attract investors, but truthfully, I can't see Lou giving up his control to answer to a board and shareholders. I keep telling him, there's no way around it with a public company, everything is subject to disclosure and transparency."

"I agree with you," Kevin said. "I can't see him answering to a board and shareholders holders either and he can be just as successful staying private."

"Time will tell," Finn said.

CHRISTMAS A FEW WEEKS LATER WAS A FLURRY OF FAMILY. FROM all outward appearance nothing had changed with Finn. He sat on the floor with his nieces and nephews and helped tear open presents, he constructed a Lego castle with them and shimmied his six-foot frame under the tree to rescue an errant train that had careened off the tracks. He helped with the dishes and changed diapers for his brother's infant before wishing a last Merry Christmas, as he and Audrey hugged them all good-bye, loaded presents into the trunk of their car, and took off for home with their secret safely guarded.

Chapter Nine

1999

"Can we come by today? There's something Audrey and I want to talk to you about."

Margo looked out the window. Sleet was pummeling the ground. It was the end of January, early on a Saturday morning. Not a day to travel. Finn sounded serious. "Is something wrong? Did you get bad news from the fertility doctors?"

"Everything's fine. Just some business decision."

"Of course. Come."

When they arrived, Finn gravitated towards the kitchen table, long the command center of the house, a sign that this was not a trivial discussion they were about to have. Every big decision from the time the children were little got made around the kitchen table. After the coffee mugs were filled and the bagels and donuts stacked on a serving dish, they sat at the table. Finn took a deep breath and began:

As he pulled into the parking lot for the last day of work before Christmas, Lou got out of his car to wait for him. It was Christmas Eve morning. Light snow was falling, painting the fields and the PARC Labs complex in a brightness that matched Finn's mood. As they walked towards the door together, trailing twin footprints in the snow, Lou casually said, "Stop by my office before you leave, Finn. I want to talk to you about the year we've had."

Finn felt happy. Ever since Artie told him about the impending offer to buy Bakers Palette, he'd had his radar up, anticipating a conversation with Lou about assuming more responsibility. He had been working at PARC Labs for almost two years. He had rotated through several departments and the timing to move forward on the business plan seemed right. As he walked to Lou's office at noon, Finn let himself dream. He went so far as to entertain the idea that Lou was going to acknowledge the success the company was enjoying in the food market, sort of an informal annual review to initiate the next phase of his assuming oversight of the company. Maybe even a bonus or finally a grant of stock in the company. That would be a nice thing to hear about on Christmas Eve. He called Audrey to let her know he might be a little later than planned. "Lou wants to talk to me about our year. I have a good feeling."

He could hear laughter as he approached the office and was surprised to find Artie, Rob, and Carl already there. Angela was there too. She had just finished arranging platters of sand-wiches and salads on the table. "Merry Christmas, Finn!" she said, as she gave him a big motherly hug. He had gotten used to Angela's shows of affection. Sometimes it made him blush when she treated him like a long-lost son come into the fold.

"I'll leave you all to your man's lunch," she said over her shoulder as she left the room, closing the door behind her.

"Come in! Come in! Grab a sandwich, before we get start-ed," Lou said as he closed a file on his desk, put it in the drawer and made his way to the buffet table. He fixed himself a plate before taking his seat behind his big oak desk. The three sons and Finn all made plates for themselves and took seats in the four chairs prearranged around the desk. Angela had decorated a balsam wreath with silver bells and a huge red bow and hung it on the window behind the desk. Remembering the scene, Finn said sarcastically, "with the sun streaming in the window illuminating Lou's head in the oval of the wreath, he looked like a portrait of himself."

Sarcasm was uncharacteristic of Finn. A little alarm went off inside Margo's chest. Finn continued, "Lou swiveled in his chair and, addressing me, said, 'I want the boys involved today. As we turn the corner in 1998, as managers of departments and future shareholders, their input on how the year has gone is important. I want us to hear it together.'

Finn was a little put off by Lou's words, *future shareholders*. That was unusual. Lou had never referred to his sons that way before, just as he didn't refer to Finn as *future president*. The hierarchy was generally low key, informal, and understood. Turning towards Artie, Lou said, "Why don't you start us, Artie. Tell us what you think about the year. How's Finn doing?"

Artie hesitated. He shifted awkwardly in his chair. Finn could not tell if Artie had been expecting the question or was taken by surprise. Suddenly, Finn felt like the meeting was turning into an annual review by committee, a committee of future shareholders, three of whom reported to him. It made him uncomfortable, but not worried. This wasn't Wall Street. Things were more casual, less formal at PARC Labs. He still hoped the meeting would culminate in the moment when they would all bask in the glow of the year's successes, before leaving for the Christmas holiday.

Artie kept it short, reiterating to his father what Finn already knew. Everything was going great. The new confectionary products were going strong. They could barely keep up with the orders. People in the industry were taking notice of and talking about the new brand. He concluded by saying, "We've had a great year. Couldn't be better."

97

Lou shifted his attention to Rob. "How about you, Rob? What do you think?"

Rob responded much the same as Artie, adding that the core pharmaceutical business continued to thrive. Since they'd purchased the new warehouse, they had been able to smoothly incorporate production and distribution of the new brand. The initial problems about space had been worked out and they were excited about developing new products that were already in the pipeline.

"That's it?" Lou asked. "No concerns from either of your perspectives?"

They shook their heads. "On the contrary." Rob said. "The year has been one of the best."

It was then Lou turned to Carl. Without hesitation, he launched into his evaluation, vehemently disagreeing with his brothers. "Finn has us moving too fast. I've already developed all our available space. There's no more room for expansion."

He stopped addressing his father and turned towards Finn accusing him of spending too much money and veering from the core pharmaceutical business into irrelevant side projects.

"I was stunned," Finn told them. "It was as though he'd thrown acid in my face. I looked at Lou, waiting for him to respond to his son. Lou wouldn't make eye contact with me. I calmed myself and prepared to refute Carl; in essence, educate him, knowing Carl did not even bother, much less know, how to read business or financial statements.

"They're not irrelevant side projects, Carl." Finn explained. They were meticulously developed expansion plans, and every decision was made with Lou's full knowledge and backing. He made clear that Bakers Palette had generated revenues north of five million dollars in its first year, while the pharmaceutical line continued to perform as it had over the last few years.

Carl cut Finn off mid-sentence. "You and my father are out of the office constantly. I can never find him. There is no more physical room to expand. We are using every inch of space. We're spending too much money on consultants. Now we have advertising and design people, and God knows who else that we don't need, taking up space and costing us money."

Carl was a speeding train, building momentum. He stood up and began to pace as he kept talking. "We need to go back to the old way of doing things, focus on the old customers and the pharmaceutical products, pull back on the expansion plans."

Finn looked at Lou. He still refused to make eye contact. He looked at Artie and Rob. They both met his gaze but looked anxious, and disgusted, but not surprised. Neither of them said a word to intercede or contradict their younger brother.

Carl continued his rant. "Now we have a great offer to sell Bakers Palette, and that's what we should do. We need to scale back. We can all make a lot of money from the sale. It's an offer too good to ignore."

Finn waited for Artie or Rob to speak up, challenge Carl. Nothing.

"Lou?" Finn said, after a few moments of gathering his thoughts. "Lou?"

Nothing. Artie broke the silence. "Dad?" Still no response from Lou.

It was clear Lou was not about to get involved in Carl's complaints, even though they completely undid the vision of the company he and Finn had been implementing for the previous two years.

"I felt nausea crawl up my chest and settle in the back of my throat," Finn told Margo and Kevin. In one dizzying moment, all the warnings about getting involved in a family business came rushing back—the coursework at Stanford, the cautions issued from his trusted cadre of classmates, the due diligence before signing on with the company, the seminars at Columbia with Lou, none had prepared him for this.

"My gut told me this was the beginning of the end," Finn said. "Lou was never going to follow through on relinquishing control of PARC Labs. What was worse, I never saw it coming. I felt powerless, as powerless as that day when I was eleven years old, and a gang of kids ambushed me in the lots and knocked me off the brand-new Schwinn bike. Do you remember? I'd saved up my allowance for months to buy it. It was everything I wanted. I never saw that bike again."

Sorrow flooded Margo. She did remember her son running in the back door of the house, unaware his forehead was bleeding, as he sobbed over the stolen red-and-white Schwinn bike he was so proud of.

"Isn't there any way you could talk this out with Lou?" Kevin asked. He removed his glasses and put them on the table, as if he might see into the situation more clearly without them.

Finn looked thoughtful and took a few seconds before responding. "Even if I could salvage Bakers Palette and fend off the sale, it's clear Lou is allowing his son to disrupt the long-range plan he had asked me to develop. I can't spend the rest of my career on such shaky ground. As the full reality hit me, I knew I had to get out of there. I got up and left the meeting and the building. When I got home, I vomited."

"Didn't anyone try to stop you?" Margo asked incredulously.

"No. Later, when I sorted it out with Audrey, I wondered if I'd been set up."

"No. Lou wouldn't do that," Margo protested.

She could see the stress on Finn's face. Audrey reached across the table and put her hand on his wrist in solidarity.

"It's hard to believe Lou didn't interject anything. Try to stop Carl." Kevin said. "Christmas Eve was over a month ago. Has he brought it up again? Apologized? Explained?"

Finn shook his head at each of the questions.

"No, I thought he might think about it over the holidays

and say something in early January about Carl's rant. That's why I waited till now to tell you. But he never brought it up." He ran his fingers through his short hair, a habit from childhood whenever he felt frustrated.

"How about Artie or Rob? Or even Carl? Has anyone mentioned it?"

"Carl is ignoring me. Artie and Rob both came by my office after the holidays. Basically, their message was, "Just forget it. It never should have happened. Carl doesn't know what he's talking about, he doesn't understand the business."

"I asked them, 'Why didn't either of you say something? Interrupt him? Give your opinion while it was happening.'

'It happened so fast. We figured my father would stop him,' Rob said. They were as shocked as Finn at the things that came out of their brother's mouth. They'd been conditioned to stick together, and knew they had Christmas dinner to get through. 'We've been talking to Lou about it since then,' Rob went on. 'He knows the two of us want things to continue as they are. It's not over yet. He hasn't signed the papers to sell Bakers Palette.'"

Hearing this, Margo took a deep breath, thinking this is where things start to settle. "So that's good for you. Artie and Rob are supporting you and trying to persuade their father," she said.

"No, not really, Mom. It's not the actual sale that has me rethinking my commitment to making a career there. It's the fact that Lou recruited me to run the company. He placed me in a position above his sons in the overall structure. For him to even entertain such a major sale, then go ahead and discuss it with his sons without even mentioning it to me, regardless of whether he goes ahead and sells it or not, is a clear signal to me that things have changed. I'd rather cut my losses and move on."

They were all silent as they took in this uncomfortable truth.

Finn asked, "Have either of you talked to them since the holidays? Have they reached out to you?"

They shook their heads. Their friends hadn't been in touch. Silence hung like a black cloud over the kitchen table.

"With all this going on, I can't believe Angela hasn't called me," Margo said.

"I wouldn't be surprised if she didn't even know what happened in that meeting, Mom. She wasn't there. I doubt Lou discussed it with her."

Finn continued haltingly, "I've been thinking about leaving, but I don't want to cause a rift in your friendship. I have these memories of us all being together when we were kids, coming in from ice hockey in their back yard and drinking hot chocolate in front of a fire in their tv room. But the thing I remember most is the four of you parents in the kitchen, laughing so hard that us kids would just roll our eyes at each other and turn up the volume on the tv. You had so much fun together. I don't want to take that away from you."

He was right. Margo didn't want to lose that shared history, the seasons she cherished and returned to, their younger selves remembered each time they were together. She didn't want to lose the future, the four of them on trips, the dinners at Lunello, the laughs, growing old together. Yet, her feelings of impending loss competed with an anger, rising like hot lava within her. It would consume her for months The internal struggle to right her wronged son attached itself like a burr in her brain.

"You have a contract with him, don't you?" Kevin asked.

"Yes, but if you're implying, I hire an attorney and try to hold him to it, I'm not going to do that. Even if I won, it would result in a contentious relationship. I have no appetite for building a career on a lawsuit."

"You're right" Kevin said. "That's no way to live."

"I can't believe Lou is going to leave it like this. Surely, he will talk with you at some point," Margo said.

"I thought so, too, Mom. There have been plenty of opportunities this whole month of January. I feel he is avoiding me. I've asked for a meeting on two occasions, and it hasn't happened. My stomach is churning every day from the undercurrents of betrayal. My trust has been destroyed."

"I can understand why you feel it's better to cut your losses and leave sooner rather than later," Kevin said, as he got up from the table and began to busy himself with refilling the coffee pot. It was as though this small act of moving around in the kitchen would relieve the tension of just sitting there, impotent as a rock, unable to do a thing to change the situation.

Margo's mind was racing, looking for some hint that this was all a mistake, an overreaction on Finn's part. What he was describing just didn't gel with what she knew and believed about Angela and Lou. Yet she knew Finn could never choose to work in an environment that was simmering with an unspoken discontent below the surface of everyday encounters. In their family, he was the peacemaker, the one who got them back on track when something was amiss. Kevin finally spoke for both of them.

"You've got to get out of there, Finn. Do what you need to do. You have our support."

"Don't worry about the friendship," Margo added. "We go back too far to let it end over this. We'll work on salvaging it." Although, at that moment, her anger at Lou was so intense, she wondered if she could keep that promise. Floodwaters of betrayal washed over her. It was their friendship that brought them into this when they recruited Finn. Now, not a word. This made the betrayal cut deeper.

"I'm going to call Angela and find out what's going on," Margo said, as she regressed to earlier years when, alike in instincts to protect their children, Angela and she would talk about their hurts, look for solutions to problems together. Hadn't Angela run onto the football field to get to Artie when as a high school freshman he lay limp under a pileup of players. In retrospect, it became one of Lou's hilarious stories, Angela barreling onto the field, pushing past coaches and medics, kneeling over her son. She intervened when her sons were hurting. Angela would understand.

"No." Finn said, from that place beyond the thoughts and plans evolving in Margo's head. "I don't want you to get involved. I'll take care of it."

Chapter Ten

1999

For the next month, each time the phone rang, Margo willed it to be Lou or Angela. Surely, they would call, explain. Her imagination went into overdrive, a mad machine spinning fantasies that played on a constant loop in her mind. The fantasy she tended to dwell on most went something like this:

It takes place on a Saturday morning. Or maybe Sunday. The four of them meet for an impromptu coffee and bagels. Maybe at Starbucks, maybe at Dunkin' Donuts. The setting is irrelevant. Lou looks nervous. That's important. Angela looks sad. In a halting voice and without his usual preemptive attempt at humor, Lou says, "I'm so sorry about what happened with Finn."

Relief floods Margo as Lou continues, "Carl was jealous of the time I spent with Finn. He came to me right before Christmas. He said he was thinking of leaving the company."

Lou looks at Angela. She's dabbing at her eyes with a tissue. Margo doesn't know if she is crying because her son is threatening to leave the company or because Lou has told her about Carl's behavior at the Christmas Eve meeting.

"I know I should have intervened at that meeting," Lou says. "It was a mistake. I'm sorry and I'm going to fix it."

And everyone lives happily ever after...

Margo's second fantasy revolves around money. Either Lou needed the money the sale of the brand would bring him, or he just plain wanted the windfall. In this fantasy, Lou has come to realize the transparency requirements for a public company are more than he will ever be ready to undertake. A sort of bird-in-hand impulse has replaced the continued expansion plan linked to going public he'd been so enthusiastic about when he recruited Finn. It is early December, three weeks prior to the Christmas Eve meeting. The family have all gathered at the house for Sunday dinner. Lou unties the apron straining around his middle and picks up the antipasto that he's been fixing in the kitchen. Salami, roasted peppers, and artichoke hearts are beautifully arranged with olives and cheeses on a white platter that once belonged to his mother. He can't wait to announce the fantastic offer to sell Bakers Palette. He grabs a bottle of champagne and pops the cork. When he has everyone's attention, he breaks the news. A chorus of "Wow's" echoes through the room. He assumes Finn will defer to his decision the way his sons have learned to do.

Margo's third fantasy was the only one that allowed her to feel empathy instead of anger at Carl. An inkling that had, throughout the years, been no more than a passing thought, grew into an epic story she told herself. There had been conversations over the years.

In the mid-eighties, Angela and she were alone in the kitchen, clearing dishes from the table after one of those ice hockey Sundays. Lou and Kevin were huddled in front of the tv in the family room, watching football. The AID's crisis was still in its infancy, and protocols for avoiding the dreaded infection were still being formulated. For the most part, it was believed an exchange of bodily fluids was the mechanism for passing the virus on. In those early days, all bodily fluids were suspect. The previous week, Margo had been facilitating a group therapy session with about eight patients at the psychiatric hospital where she worked. In a moment of desperation, an AID's patient in the group, hospitalized for anxiety and depression, had turned towards her as the group leader and spontaneously thrown his arms around her neck as he broke down in tears. "I knew I couldn't push him away," she confided to Angela, "but at the same time I realized his tears were bodily fluids that were being transferred onto me. I froze in fear. I consoled him and gradually unpeeled him from my neck the best I could, but the thought of those tears brushing against my cheek is still lurking in the back of my mind."

As Angela took in what Margo said, she suddenly turned sheet white and lost her balance. She had to sit down, and Margo could tell Angela was more frightened than she was. The epidemic was alarming to every mother as it ravished the gay population, and Margo's mind flew to Carl. She dismissed the suspicion, but the seed had been planted.

More recently, the morning after Finn's wedding in 1994, devoid of make-up, their day-after hair limp as they relaxed around the breakfast table, Angela said wistfully, "I wish Carl would find a girl, someone to marry, settle down like the other boys."

Lou downplayed her concern. "Well, she would have to be as neat and fastidious as he is. Who could put up with those closets full of designer shoes and cashmere sweaters?"

"There are lots of women out there who would love that," Angela retorted. "Better than the khakis and sneakers in your closet."

"Well, he's happy spending his weekends antiquing and

poking around county fairs while his brothers go grocery shopping or visit their in-laws. He likes his freedom. Let him be."

Now Margo pulled these little threads together and wove her third fantasy. In it, Carl is attracted to Finn and that's the problem.

She knew a friendship had been developing between them as Carl helped Finn with his woodworking at the house. In fantasy number three, when Carl finds himself attracted to Finn, he knows he needs to change the situation. He could never confess this to his father. Even Margo knew that. Angela was another story. She would have listened and supported her son in whatever he needed to do to manage his life. Margo respected that. She could understand Angela doing anything to keep her youngest son close and safe in the orbit of their family and their business.

During the active days of this fantasy, Margo once asked Finn if he thought Carl was gay. "I have no idea. Why would you even ask that?"

She didn't answer him.

Her fourth fantasy and perhaps the most disturbing but the easiest for her to discard, was that Finn just didn't measure up to Lou's expectations: Lou saw her son as a drain on the business. He wasn't working out. Hiring him had been a mistake. Finn had some massive flaw that Margo was oblivious to and, as good friends, Lou and Angela didn't want to tell Kevin and her some awful truth about their son. They were protecting their old friends. Like a cat playing with yarn, one by one, she knotted her fantasies into a tangle she couldn't unravel.

"Has Lou said anything to you?" She'd ask Finn periodically, as winter limped across the calendar, and she clawed her way from one fantasy to another.

"No, he acts as though nothing has changed."

Margo was in the kitchen Sunday morning making coffee when the back door banged, and in walked Finn. It was late April, and he and Audrey had stayed over on Saturday night after attending a wedding. Finn was best man for an old high school friend and the wedding was in the neighborhood.

"What are you doing up so early? I thought you were still asleep."

"I went for a run. I followed my old route through the neighborhood. It was great, it's a gorgeous day out there," Finn said, as his dog nipped at his legs in greeting. He pulled a chair away from the table, sat down, and stroked the dog's head. "That coffee smells so good."

Margo poured each of them a cup and joined him. She could sense it was a rare opportunity, alone time with one of her adult children.

"So how is everything going?"

"Nothing different at PARC Labs, if that's what you mean. I go in each day. I do my job. Artie and Rob tell me they are still working on their father to hold off on selling Bakers Palette. Carl avoids me. We haven't had any interaction since that meeting on Christmas Eve."

"Have you tried to ask Lou directly about what's going on, what's changed?"

"I've gotten proactive in asking for assurances about where we are headed, assurances about increasing my responsibilities in preparation for the presidency, as we agreed to before I came on board. Lou's answer is 'Be patient, nothing has changed,' but the reality is, for me everything has changed. Lou and Angela are going on a cruise next month, and he asked me to run things. That will give me a little breathing room."

Still stroking the dog's head, Finn said, "I can't believe I didn't see all this coming. It's the biggest mistake I ever made." Margo could hear the defeat in his voice as she watched his animation from the run deplete in front of her. "It reminds me of when I was in high school and those perverted telephone calls kept coming in every night. Do you remember?"

"Vaguely," Margo said, as a picture materialized of her tousle-haired, scared fourteen-year-old son, his overgrown bare feet sticking out of his pajamas when, in the middle of the night, he held the telephone to his ear, repeating over and over, "Who are you? Who are you?"

Finn continued, "I hadn't thought about it in years, but this whole affair with PARC Labs is bringing it all back."

"I don't understand. They're totally different."

"Not to me. They're both instances of someone pretending to be my friend, while secretly disliking me and working against me; in each case, I am oblivious, living in an alternate reality. What does that say about me?"

"I think it says more about Lou than you," she answered haltingly, as she began to see the parallels.

The first call had come in on the "teen phone," a second line installed to free the house phone for three teen-agers vying for telephone time with their friends. There were house rules. Among them, no calls after ten-thirty at night. When the phone rang after midnight one school night, Margo jumped out of bed and answered. A male voice asked for Finn, "It's an emergency." Taken in by the young plaintive voice, she broke her own rule and fetched him. And so, it began. A series of calls, the essence of which was, "I'm watching you," "I'm going to get you," issued from a mouth laced with threats and perversion.

Finn had been enrolled as a sophomore in his new school. He was happy. He'd made new friends, loved his classes and teachers, ran track, and worked with the stage crew building sets for the school productions. Everything was going great; just like the past two years at PARC Labs.

The calls continued. It wasn't easy to identify the culprit who was terrorizing Finn and by extension, the family. There was no caller ID, no mobile phones in the seventies. The telephone company was unable to trace a call unless the order came through the police department. The police urged them to wait it out. "Our experience is that this guy will eventually stop and move on to someone else."

Margo lived in fear as the calls continued. A stranger was stalking her son and knew details of his life. She and Kevin took turns listening in on an extension, hoping for the caller to drop some clue. Eventually, he did. He referred to an incident in Finn's math class. That was big. It narrowed the search and alleviated some of the terror. It was another teen, one whose voice had already changed to that of a man. The school administration acted swiftly. The police got involved and ordered the telephone company to put a trace on the phone.

It didn't take long for the telephone company to identify the number and report the household name of the listing to the school. The caller was a fellow student who sat near Finn in geometry. Finn knew him as just another kid in the class, a seemingly nice kid. Finn was shocked to learn he was the threatening caller. There had been no signs that the boy even knew who Finn was. The boy's parents were contacted, and the student was immediately suspended. The calls ceased. The case was sent to a panel of citizens who arbitrated juvenile cases outside the court. Margo and Kevin had input but asked only that the boy receive mandatory counseling, which did become a condition of his parole. The school, on the other hand, expelled him.

After it was over, Margo rarely thought of it again. Now, she was learning how the experience had seeded itself deep in her son's psyche. The current unmasking of Carl's disdain and Lou's abiding it sent Finn tumbling back to his fourteen-year-old self. It offered him proof that he couldn't trust his own judgement. Convinced he had some major inadequacy more potent than anything he had accomplished since, his self-esteem plummeted, his confidence shattered.

The sadness Margo felt hearing that her once confident, high-achieving son was reduced to a shadow of himself by her friends, gave way to an anger that wanted revenge. *Lou can't get away with this,* she thought. Remembering how she had interceded, encouraging Finn to consider Lou's recruitment effort three years earlier, turned her sorrow to a teeth-gritting rage.

In the weeks that followed, Finn continued to go into work each day. He did not approach Lou when he returned from the cruise and Lou did not approach him. He knew, from Artie, the deal to sell Bakers Palette was still on the table, and he still had not been asked for his input.

On some level Margo clung to a belief that if the four of them could just get together, the situation would make its way naturally into the conversation. She may not like what she heard, or be able to change it, but the not knowing was like a worm in an apple, eating at her, bite by bite.

Chapter Eleven

1999

F inn and Audrey were waiting for them in the yard on a sunny Father's Day in June. Laddie, their Golden retriever, jumped up to greet Margo and Kevin even before they climbed out of the car. After the initial hugs, Finn said, "We have so much to show you. Come see the garden first, we planted tomatoes and cucumbers, beans, and even kohlrabi."

"Kohlrabi," Margo said. "Who do you think you are, Grandpa?

"I knew you'd appreciate that," Finn said, as they warmed to the family memory of grandpa inventing a vegetable no one had ever heard of before, when Finn was ten and learned to love gardening from him. "Now that I'm a landowner, I'm reinstating the gardening tradition," as if his little backyard plot was a midwestern farm.

"Come see the way we got my grandmother's dry sink to fit in the kitchen," Audrey said, as they entered the house, "and look at our new stove, five burners!" In the dining room, Finn said, "Close your eyes. I want to turn on the light switch, so you get the full effect of this." There, before them, was the *piece de resistance*, wainscoting Finn had cut from raw oak and painstakingly sanded, stained, and installed.

"It's gorgeous," Margo said, as Kevin and she drew their palms over the satin finish. After the tour, they sat down to a brunch of quiche and salad and the bread Audrey had baked earlier that day. Then, as if unable to contain themselves a minute longer, they looked at each other and Finn blurted, "We have something good to tell you."

Since Margo's preoccupation with Finn's situation at PARC Labs was always lurking in the shadows of her mind, her first thought was one of relief, as she anticipated hearing the whole fiasco had been resolved and it had all been a big misunderstanding.

But no, she realized, it wasn't PARC Labs at all.

"We're going to have a baby," Audrey announced.

Margo screeched her joy. Tears rose in Kevin's eyes. After four years of fertility treatments, high hopes, and disappointments, this *maybe* baby, the miracle they had dreamed of, was happening. As they listened to every detail of the previous six weeks, thoughts of PARC Labs receded like passing headlights on a country road.

Later, as Laddie let it be known he wanted out, Finn fastened the leash around his neck and he and Kevin went for a walk. It was then that Audrey shared. "Finn looks and acts fine but his confidence in himself is still shattered. He feels going to work for Lou caused him to lose three years of building his career. It's made him doubt himself, shaken him."

"I was hoping he would start to feel better, sort things out, while Lou and Angela were away on the cruise," Margo said.

"Not so far as I can see," Audrey said as she rubbed her hands protectively over her belly. "He told me he feels obsolete."

"Oh no. He shouldn't feel that way," Margo said, as though

her words of protest could erase her son's feeling. "Why does he feel obsolete?"

Audrey took a breath. "When he made the decision to move to PARC Labs three years ago, the dot-com bubble was still raging. There were lots of opportunities, but now, it's unclear…"

Margo understood. At the time Finn made his move, investors were pumping money into internet-based start-ups. It was a time of frenetic growth as the internet became the vehicle of the future. Some of these startups would fail as quickly as they emerged. Others were destined to become the engines of the future.

Audrey continued, "Maybe I shouldn't have told you this. But the good news is Finn has his antenna up for making a move. He's put out the word that he might be ready to leave PARC Labs. He hasn't done anything formal, like getting in touch with a headhunter. He's quietly gathering information. Three years ago, he was well-positioned to be in that market, but now, he isn't so sure."

"How do you feel about moving now that you're pregnant?

"We've talked about it. We can do it. No matter what, I'll continue with my doctor down here."

On the drive home Margo thought about her conversation with Audrey. With a baby coming the situation was more complicated. Instead of being settled they were faced with upending their lives again. She asked Kevin if the topic of PARC Labs had come up on his walk with Finn. It hadn't. "Finn talked about nothing but the baby and how happy they are," he said.

"Did you ask him if Bakers Palette was sold?"

"No, he would have told me if it was something he wanted to discuss. You have to leave it alone, Margo. This is his life. He'll figure it out."

She could not unscramble the Lou she knew, the one who

rode the subway with Angela and her on their way home from the School for Brides almost forty years ago, the one who helped Angela's father shower every day for weeks after his stroke, the one who drove through a snowstorm to help his son with a college paper, the brilliant chemist who forced himself to participate in a dinner ritual of eating monkey brains in China, so as not to offend his hosts. She could find no logic in his being unaware of Finn's feelings, and by extension Kevin's and hers, and refusing to address them.

She even considered Finn had missed something. That he was wrong in his evaluation of the situation. No one is perfect. A simple conversation with Lou could produce an ah-ha! moment—when everything would return to normal.

The Fourth of July weekend was coming up, the holiday their two families had spent together when it was still possible to haul the children with them on family outings. It was a good excuse to meet, renew an old tradition. She called Angela and invited them to the house, but once again, they opted for the halfway restaurant. Margo convinced herself the conversation she wanted to have would evolve at that dinner and this whole unfortunate situation would be put to rest.

As they drove the familiar route to Lunello, she found herself clearing her throat repeatedly, a telltale sign she was nervous.

Kevin heard it too. "What are you nervous about?"

"I think tonight will be the night we find out what happened."

"How so? What's going to make tonight any different from our last dinner?"

"I know by now Lou and Angela are aware of the pregnancy. It's got to come up. I think I can segue into asking what happened once we're talking about the pregnancy."

"And if you can't segue?"

"Then I'll just casually bring it up, something like, I understand Carl was very upset with Finn at the Christmas Eve meeting. Is everything okay?"

"You can't do that, for two reasons. First, you promised Finn you'd leave it alone. And beyond that, it would be asking, why was your kid mean to my kid? My God, you never even interfered like that when the kids were little."

Kevin was right. "Will you support me if I can manage to get on the topic in an indirect way?"

"Yes, but think hard. I doubt you will feel any better for asking."

"Finn's on the brink of altering his whole life again. Maybe that doesn't have to happen."

"How are you going to ask for information indirectly?"

"I'll think of something. I've been trained as a therapist to delicately probe for information in an indirect way, go in the back door. So, I'll wait for an opportunity to present itself."

Margo and Kevin arrived at Lunello first. Even before Angela and Lou sat down at the table, Lou's voice echoed across the room, to them, and everyone else in the restaurant, "Congratulations. I thought your son was going to explode when he came into the office and announced they were pregnant. It's perfect timing," Lou continued, as he proceeded to adjust his chair and unfolded his napkin. "They're settled in the house, and they have one of the best obstetricians in the area, the same one my daughters-in-law use. I knew it would happen, I told Finn months ago, you just have to be patient. Give it time."

Margo's ears perked up. Patient. Wasn't that what he said when Finn asked for assurances within the business? She'd found her segue: "Yes, you're right, a lot of things take patience …" and then she faltered. Couldn't do it. She'd promised Finn she would stay out of it. They were all acting as if that

Christmas Eve meeting had never happened. Lou had just affirmed that the pregnancy was perfect timing. Almost seven months had gone by, and he seemed to have no idea that Finn was quietly contemplating a move. It was obvious Lou believed the Christmas Eve meeting was behind him and that Finn had yielded to his decision to sell Bakers Palette and change course with the business, just as Margo, in that moment, was changing course with her resolve to get her question answered.

Kevin tried to help her. "How are things at the company?"

"Good. Busy as ever. We're ramping up with new orders. Everything's running smoothly. We're taking the house at Rehoboth Beach for the month of August and your son will be manning the ship. I left him at the helm when we took a cruise a few weeks ago."

"Yes, we heard. Finn told us you were on a cruise."

Margo was sure there were other details about the trip recounted that night which receded into some part of her brain she could no longer access. What remained etched in her mind, like some ancient myth, was a story they told about a woman they had met. Margo even remembered her name, Lenore. She was traveling alone. Her twenty-two-year-old daughter had recently died after a short illness.

"We felt so bad for her," Angela said. "She was crying all the time. Other travelers were not bothering with her. She was so isolated. We cancelled a few of the shore excursions so we could keep her company on deck. We had dinner with her every night and listened when she needed to talk. We tried to take care of her."

My God, Margo thought. Who does that? Who gives up days and days on a cruise ship to help a total stranger? Here were their friends, the people they'd known for forty years, exquisitely sensitive to the pain of a stranger. Compelled to put themselves out to alleviate Lenore's pain, they remained oblivious to the distress Finn was experiencing as a direct result of their actions. Even as these thoughts collided in her mind, Angela was extracting a package from the oversized purse she still carried. Over the years, they often joked about their dueling handbags filled with cans of apple juice and ace bandages and spare keys and extra sweatshirts. But those days were gone. Margo could see the wrapping on the package Angela was pulling out of the bag. It bore the cruise line's logo. "Here is a little something I brought back for you," she said, as she leaned across the table and handed her a replacement for the Belleek salt-and-peppershaker Margo had dropped and broken years ago. Margo had forgotten about it. Angela had remembered.

They talked all around the meeting that had unsettled Finn's life: the weather, the snowstorms, the flu, the horse Artie's wife had recently acquired, the grandchildren, the condition of a mutual acquaintance's back, the updated offerings on the menu, the addition of new oil paintings of Italy on the wall. The subject of Finn melted like ice on a hot stove.

As the conversation exhausted itself, Lou gestured to the waiter for the check, implying he was ending the evening. It was only then, affecting that familiar sheepish posture and smile that Margo had come to affectionately associate with a humility he didn't possess, he lowered his shoulders, making himself smaller and averting his eyes, to announced, "We just set up an endowment for scholarships at my old high school, St. Thomas More, in Brooklyn. I figure my education got me to where I am today, and with the business doing so well, it's time to pay it forward."

Margo's head began to swim. Dizziness engulfed her. *The business doing so well,* Lou had said. Was this a second opportunity to segue? Ask about Bakers Palette? Yet the enormity of Lou and Angela's generosity disarmed her. It dwarfed her preoccupation, like a small shell under water, carried off in the current. Despite her seemingly wronged son, how could she sit in judgement of a man who was endowing scholarships for needy students? What kind of a person was she?

As they sat there, absorbing Lou's announcement, Angela was quiet. She began to rub her eyes. She suddenly looked weary and embarrassed. She hoisted her purse from under the table and said, "Let's save that conversation for another day, Lou, I'm tired. It's time to go home."

Lou ignored her.

The conversation took a turn towards Lou's beneficence. As Margo listened, it took all her energy to keep from spitting out, "Your windfall is not luck, my friend! What a lovely thing to do after filling your coffers with the thirty pieces of silver with which you betrayed my son."

Unlike Margo, Kevin had moved on, and was congratulating Lou on his generosity.

Their friends seemed blind to what had transpired for Finn. From their *everything is great* attitudes nothing had changed for them. Margo knew that by avoiding the subject, they were conveying nothing had changed for them either.

Yet, she didn't trust herself to acknowledge the event at the center of her angst without making things worse. What's more, she had promised her son she wouldn't bring it up. She feared an argument or a standoff that would completely end the friendship, which Finn would have taken on as another failure. On balance, the shared family history and her respect for Finn's wishes trumped her ability to speak her mind. Once again, the evening ended with the bubble of the unspoken intact—the couples' relationship surviving, her son's future blowing in the wind.

It is said that the circumstances of one's first experience with death will echo in future experiences. Margo had come to believe it is no different when confronted with the loss of a friendship, another kind of death.

Recurring images of Anne Marie came to her during those months of anger at Lou. Anne Marie was her friend in first grade, at the insulated elementary school where everyone knew everyone else, and the only thing to fear was a nun with a penchant for discipline. A black-and-white photo survived that year. In it, Anne Marie and Margo and a few other seven-year-old students in winter coats, are shyly standing alongside a Christmas tree in the back of the classroom. Margo had no memory of the event, like so many moments in life that time dissipates and folds into the ether. Yet the photo contained a slice of time depicted in Anne Marie's long red curls, freckled face, and Mona Lisa smile.

Anne Marie lived with her mother in a row apartment above a laundromat, where the washing machines and dryers groaned and shook beneath them, and the elevated train line cast long shadows on the red brick building all day long. Stores lined the sidewalk underneath the steel girders supporting the tracks that ran for miles along Liberty Avenue. This area was named City Line, because it was where New York's Kings County ended, and Queens County began.

As little girls holding hands on the way home from school, Anne Marie and Margo passed Joe's Butcher, the Economy Shop with its bins of underwear lined up on the sidewalk, and Nathan's Bar & Grill where the scent of franks and sauerkraut were an invitation wafting through the open door. There was Woolworth's, the five-and-dime store that drew children like mice to cheese. Open counters of gummy bears and Tootsie Rolls and Good & Plenty beckoned. Woolworth's was where their secret bonding, never confessed to anyone else, took place. Standing in their navy knee socks, lusting after penny candy, hearts thumping, they each lifted a sweet prize from the candy case and slipped it into the pocket reserved for rosary beads in their daily uniform. They were partners in crime. They were comrades forever.

On many days, Margo went with Anne Marie into that apartment above the laundromat to get her mother's permission to go out and play after school. She followed behind her, up the narrow staircase and into the kitchen, through the row of railroad rooms and into a dark bedroom. It was there that Ann Mare's mother, still as a doll under a blue quilt, her white face all but swallowed by the white pillows, lay dying. The curtains were always closed against the faces in the train windows, where riders had a bird's eye view of the bedroom. No daylight entered the room. There was only the roar of the train as it careened past every four minutes, sure as death, speeding to deliver commuters at the next station.

Margo stood a few feet behind Anne Marie, waiting for her mother to nod her assent, waiting for her to inhale her daughter's redheaded presence. They ran down the stairs for the short walk to Margo's house, where her mother and grandmother waited with chocolate milk and Oreo cookies.

One day, Anne Marie was gone. Simply gone. Lost to Margo, the way Ann Marie's father was lost to her, when he never came home from the war. The nuns at school said she had moved. But no one seemed to know where. For months Margo hesitated each time she walked past the laundromat, half expecting to catch a glimpse of long red curls bouncing through the narrow doorway that led from the second-floor apartment. It is almost half a century later, and sometimes Margo thinks she is still looking for Anne Marie.

So, Margo is careful with friendships. She avoids confrontation. Despite her sense of unfinished business between the four friends, she defaulted and let her sense of injustice and anger smolder rather than stoke a fire.

Driving home, it started to rain. Her head pounded as she replayed the evening in her mind. Alone with Kevin, she couldn't contain her anger. "They must have sold Bakers Palette to be able to make such a huge donation. Why didn't they just come out and say that, rather than make no mention of it, as though the money had fallen from a tree?"

"To link it directly to what Finn created at PARC Labs would have opened the door to the conversation you want to have, the one they are avoiding," Kevin said.

"Do you think Finn knows it was sold? He's never mentioned it."

"He probably knows and is still figuring out what to do. You know his pattern, reveal the details after a problem is solved. My guess is the only reason he shared any of this with us is because he feels responsible for the impact on our friendship with Lou and Angela."

As they drove up the highway sheets of rain strained the wipers and blurred the roadway.

Caution warned Margo to end the conversation and let Kevin concentrate on his driving. As she withdrew into herself, random thoughts came unfiltered into her mind — *Reserve thy judgement...* a phrase she discovered in her high school English class. It had remained a part of her ever since. It seemed an easy admonition at the time, but now...

It was the semester of *Hamlet*. Sister Leonita noiselessly padded across the room in her sensible black shoes, all but hidden under her long black robe. Wooden rosary beads, with a large silver cross, were fastened at her waist and slow danced in the folds of her robe with every step she took. Her very presence quieted the chatter of thirty-five girls, even before the bell rang, and a predictable hush settled over classrooms and hallways alike.

The assignment, on which the final grade was based, was to choose a personally meaningful excerpt from *Hamlet*, memorize it, and recite it to the class along with an explanation of why you chose it. Reading Shakespeare was a daunting task. Margo struggled with the old English while the anticipation of standing before the class to speak caused hives to erupt on her back.

The scent of spring filled the classroom and a fine layer of pollen turned the windowsills yellow. The trees along the sidewalks of Brooklyn bloomed, as did each of the adolescent girls, memorizing their excerpts and pouring their souls into their presentations. Now all these years later, the lines she had memorized pounded in her mind like the rain on the windshield. "Reserve thy judgement," came unbidden, and with it the whole of Polonius' speech.

Give thy thoughts no tongue,
Nor any unproportion'd thought his act.
Be thou familiar, but by no means vulgar.
The friends thou hast, and their adoption tried,
Grapple them to thy soul with hoops of steel;

Give every man thine ear, but few thy voice:
Take each man's censure but reserve thy judgement.

Margo's rising anger fought with her better angels as the car plowed through the thrashing rain.

THAT SEPTEMBER, ONE OF HIS FRIENDS FROM BUSINESS SCHOOL contacted Finn. Peter had been among the group Finn confided in before signing on with Lou. Aware things had blown up for Finn at PARC Labs, Peter had information about a new internet start-up retail company looking for a CEO whose qualifications matched Finn's. "They are looking to take it public," Peter told Finn. "Call them."

Just like that, Finn learned he wasn't obsolete.

Unlike the extended six months due diligence he took to consider Lou's offer, this opportunity was happening now. It was a gamble, like most business ventures. For Finn, getting out from under the mantle of a family business, more than compensated for all that it would entail to make a change.

Audrey didn't blink. "Go for it," she encouraged.

Finn signed a contract on a Friday in October and gave Lou two weeks' notice the following Monday.

"How did Lou react?" Margo asked, secretly hoping the announcement prompted a discussion on all that had taken place in the previous months.

"Neither surprise nor regret. He didn't try to change my mind. He wished me luck and told me, 'No hard feelings.'"

"Interesting, no hard feelings about what?" Margo asked sarcastically. "Your resignation or what he did that forced you to resign?"

"Let it go, Mom."

"Just one more question. Did he ask where you were going?"

"No. I think he was relieved. I'm sure he thought I was going to regret it."

TWO WEEKS LATER, FINN BEGAN COMMUTING TO MANHATTAN. In a frenzy of activity, a for sale sign was installed at the front of the house, the last corner of woodwork mitered, the radial arm saw unplugged from the basement outlet. Boxes of dishes and bedding lay like sleeping cats waiting for the movers to load onto a truck for the trip to a hastily purchased house near Manhattan. Once again, Finn carried the painting of the New York skyline out of his office. Audrey gave her obstetrician her new address. She was eight weeks from her January delivery date when they left South Jersey and the shattered dream it represented.

Weeks later, Margo watched the mail for Angela's Christmas card. Sure enough, it arrived early in December, "Dearest Margo and Kevin," followed by "Let's get together soon." Just like always. Lou's "no hard feelings" to Finn echoed in the silver bells glittering on the card.

A new decade stretched before them.

Chapter Twelve

2000-2001

With Finn settled, Margo's anger gave way to gratitude that he had successfully extracted himself from this misstep in his career. What's more, he had his self-esteem back. Her bad feelings dried up like a puddle in the sun and the need to undo what she perceived as the wrong inflicted on her son, no longer took up valuable real estate in her mind. Yet a curiosity about Carl's behavior, and Lou's going along with it, occasionally surfaced like incense on the altar of righteousness.

Margo reached out to Angela after the holidays and in April they met at Lunello for their long overdue holiday dinner. "We received a beautiful birth announcement from Finn and Audrey when the baby was born. A boy! I was so sure they were having a girl," Lou boomed enthusiastically as soon as they sat down at the table.

Margo was surprised at first to learn Finn had sent an announcement, then realized she shouldn't have been. Finn was not one to hold grudges.

When Finn's name came up, she held her breath, waiting

for one of them to ask, How's Finn doing in his new job? Where did he land?

She had prepared her answer: He's doing great. He's managing a public offering for Cordelia, (a company she knew Lou would recognize). She was even prepared to throw in some impressive numbers, related to the public offering, but she never got the chance. The waiter chose that moment to announce the menu, and the conversation morphed to artichoke hearts and clams oreganata. It seemed the disruption of her son's life had been relegated to a footnote in their friendship.

Dinner was pleasant enough. "How's business?" Kevin asked at one point.

"Better than ever." They learned the Romano children were all driving Porches. Lou, as he lathered his bread with butter added, "I'm sticking with BMW's. This body getting in and out of a Porsche could be a dangerous affair."

"Are you still planning to take the business public?" Kevin asked. Lou either didn't hear the question or chose not to answer but took that moment to launch into their purchase of a weekend getaway apartment in Manhattan.

"It's small, but we will have a pullout couch, and you two can come and spend weekends with us."

Margo looked at Kevin across the table. His eyes were laughing as they met her wide-eyed look of disbelief. Lou had not only short-circuited her plan to brag about Finn's success at Cordelia's. Now she and Kevin found themselves celebrating Lou's purchase of a New York apartment to which they had an open invitation.

On the drive home Margo ventured, "What do you think about their silence about Finn, other than acknowledging the baby announcement? Their disinterest in whether he landed on his feet or not?"

"I suspect Lou already knew what you were dying to tell

him. Remember how he trolled the internet and followed Finn from afar before approaching us when he wanted to recruit him.

He reads *The Wall Street Journal;* he follows the markets. He followed Finn's career once before. I imagine he's aware of what Finn's doing and chose not to bring it up. He likes to be top-dog and may not have relished sharing the spotlight."

"What about Angela?"

"That's your department. What's your take?"

"I think it's different for Angela. Sometimes I wonder if she even knows about Carl's outburst on Christmas Eve." There was a certain innocence about Angela that Margo didn't think her friend could manufacture if she had known.

"If Lou or one of the three boys did tell her," Margo said, "I imagine she would have been upset. But to acknowledge to us that Carl was out of line would feel like a betrayal of her son. I can't blame her for that. On the other hand, if she doesn't know, she may believe Finn just up and quit PARC Labs. Maybe she feels betrayed by Finn, and by extension, us, and doesn't want to confront us for the same reason I have been unable to confront them."

"I can't imagine she doesn't know. She works there. She must be aware of Bakers Palette being sold and the windfall of money that followed."

"But she may not have realized the residual effects that change of course had on Finn."

"Well, whatever we speculate, we may never know. Can you live with that?" Kevin asked.

"Yes. It does look like our relationship has survived."

On some level, Margo still believed her curiosity would eventually be satisfied. Perhaps some weekend when they visited the New York apartment, took in a show, had breakfast together in their pajamas, it would surface—just one more story to reminisce about in their shared history. But all urgency was gone. It was no longer a need, just a curiosity, no different from that which prompted her to follow stories in the newspaper, to understand what initiated events, make sense of the world: why the mother abandoned her child, why the school expelled the student, why the car bomber planted a device. Not a lot different from the curiosity she felt exploring stories clients brought to her, as together they unraveled the hurt at the root of their depression or anxieties. That night as April rain let loose from the clouds and they hugged goodbye under Lunello's green awning, they were each in their own way trying to recreate the closeness they once shared.

IT WAS MID-DECEMBER, EIGHT MONTHS SINCE THEIR LAST meeting, when Margo realized the early Christmas card with its "Dearest Margo and Kevin" salutation had not arrived. A slight foreboding erupted within her, as though her gut knew something ominous. She decided to post her card to them, days before her usual last-minute mailing to everyone else, as a secret prompt to initiate Angela's card, with its "let's get together over the holidays," scrawled in her big looping generous handwriting. Like a little kid waiting for a sign from Santa, each day Margo watched the mail. No card. She convinced herself it was just lost in the holiday mail.

In February of 2001, Kevin and she were travelling back and forth from Washington, D.C., on a regular basis. Maura, who lived in D.C., was pregnant with twins and had been put on bedrest. The route took them right past Angela and Lou's exit on the New Jersey Turnpike. Each time they drove by, a sense of nostalgia filled Margo. Months had passed since they had all been together. With Finn's life back on track, a desire to reignite the good times, to salvage a future with Lou and Angela, far exceeded the embers of her former anger. They had almost forty years invested in the friendship. It was worth a phone call.

"Ma-argo," Angela said in surprise when she reached her at the office. "It's so good to hear from you." Relief surged through Margo. *She's missed me as much as I've missed her,* she thought. She told Angela about Maura's pregnancy and their frequent trips to D.C., that brought them within miles of Angela and Lou's home in South Jersey. "I thought perhaps we could meet some Sunday night when we are passing on the Turnpike on our way home."

"They were busy but...yes...love to get together...talk to Lou...call you back..."

Angela called back as promised and explained they go to six o'clock Mass at their church every Sunday evening. Their Sunday morning was taken up with cooking the sauce for Sunday afternoon dinner with the boys and their families. "Sunday is a busy day, but why don't you meet us at St. Augustine's, and we can go to dinner after Mass?" It wasn't quite what Margo had in mind, but she was happy they were finally going to see each other again.

MARGO AND KEVIN ARRIVED EARLY AND FOUND SEATS IN THE back of the church. They heard Lou's voice greeting people before they saw him a few minutes later. Lou kissed Margo and shook Kevin's hand. Angela gave her a hug and whispered, "Come with us. We like to sit in the front."

Observing their friends' heads bowed over the gilt-edged prayer books was something Margo had never witnessed before. So different from the irreverent Lou making jokes and poking fun during Rob's memorable Greek wedding or as tourists visiting cathedrals in France. It was obvious by the number of people who went out of their way to greet them or whisper something that made them smile, they were at the center of their church community. When did they become so devout, Margo wondered? After Mass, Margo and Kevin lingered on the fringes of the crowd in the vestibule of the church while Lou and Angela spoke to the priest. Three other couples joined them, and after the priest departed, Angela, by way of introduction, extended her arm to pull Margo and Kevin into the little group, saying, "This is Margo and Kevin, friends from way back in Brooklyn. They were passing through. Okay if they join us for dinner?"

Margo felt tears welling up as the intimate reunion she had tried to orchestrate devolved into a church social.

They made their way to a neighborhood restaurant where Angela, Lou, and the three other couples shared their local lives. Once again, Margo and Kevin felt like outsiders, extras; worse for having attempted this rendezvous. Margo vowed no matter how often their trips to Maura took them past the Princeton exit on the Turnpike, she would never again suggest they meet up spontaneously. She had no way of knowing as they said good-bye that evening and Angela whispered, "Let's get together again soon, it's been way too long," that this was the moment before the moment, whether by default or by design, their couples' relationship ended.

Maura's twins were born in late June and Margo called Angela and excitedly left word of the birth. Angela never called back. The summer came and went.

September 11, 2001. Margo was getting ready to leave the house to see a client. A frantic friend called. "Turn on the tv. A plane just hit the World Trade Center." She turned the set on just in time to see a second plane crash into the second tower. She knew, like everyone else who witnessed it, downtown New York City would be a war zone. As the scene registered in her brain she gasped, "Finn! I have to reach him. He works downtown. His building is about a mile away."

"Go," her friend said.

She hung up and dialed Finn's number and held her breath until he answered.

"A plane just hit the World Trade Center! You need to get out of the city."

"What? Calm down Mom, I'm looking out the window. It's quiet here."

The words were barely out of his mouth when she heard someone burst into Finn's office, shouting the unbelievable news. At the same time the screech of sirens in the streets below echoed through the phone.

"Okay. Just heard, got to go, talk later."

She had no way of knowing then, how many mother's sons and daughters were making that same frantic promise to "talk later," and would never be able to keep it.

"Promise me you will get out of the city," Margo blurted in panic as she watched smoke billowing from the towers on the tv screen.

"I'm a senior person here, Mom. I've got to help evacuate the building, See to all our employees. I'll come when I can." He hung up the phone.

All day the tv played a continual loop of death and destruction as another plane hit the Pentagon, and a fourth was brought down in a field in Pennsylvania. It was during this vigil, the hours of no contact or information from Finn, that the old anger, whipped by the flames of a terrorist attack, reached all the way back to Lou. Although she knew it made no sense, with all the unreasonable blame fear can generate, the desire for Finn to be safely ensconced in southern New Jersey, out of harm's way, morphed into a reason to blame Lou.

Around eleven that night Finn got home. Having safely evacuated his building, he'd made his way by foot the three miles uptown to the George Washington Bridge and joined the caravan of commuters trekking out of Manhattan.

Knowing how close they were to New York and the likelihood of Kevin or one of their children commuting to New York City that day, friends from as far away as Seattle called, "Are you and the family okay?" Angela was the one Margo wanted to tell how terrified she was, waiting to hear from Finn as the news got bleaker and bleaker, how scared she was three days later, when his twins were born prematurely. But Angela never called. Not in September, not in October, not in November, not in December.

THAT DECEMBER, MARGO SENT WHAT WOULD BE HER LAST Christmas card to Angela and Lou. It was not reciprocated.

In January, Kevin received a certified letter from Tom Olsen, PARC Labs accountant and co-director, terminating his accountant consulting contract with the company. The explanation: "New ventures have prompted us to engage a firm geographically closer to our headquarters."

"I can't say I'm surprised," Kevin told Margo a few days later, after his attempt to reach out to Lou was met with silence. "But it still hurts. I keep remembering that day when we were packing up the station wagon at their house and Lou offered to be one of my early clients. Lou even stuck by me when I had to reorganize on my own after Will Wilkins disappeared and I went in for alcohol treatment. Now, this letter without a personal word from Lou. It feels very final."

Margo's hurt flared like an inflamed joint. She asked herself, why did they dismiss us? Cut us off? We were the ones who were wronged.

She had long understood that anger and hurt are linked, like opposite sides of a coin. Where there is one you will find the other. Yet her feelings brought on by this latest slight produced a different kind of hurt. It was not a return to her original anger over the way Finn had been treated. His righting his life had dissipated that. This was a fresh hurt born out of being ignored and subtracted from Angela and Lou's life. Yet she knew it had to be connected to what had gone before.

Ruminating took her in circles. She knew Lou had secretly followed Finn's career once before. She imagined him doing so again, knowing of Finn's success, and having no interest in hearing about it from her or Kevin. Or perhaps Lou simply didn't care about what was happening in her son's life, the son he had vowed to treat as one of his own. She tried to tease apart what she really wanted; to simply resume the friendship, go on as if nothing had happened, to 'get even' with Lou, by gloating about her son taking another company public, or to have her curiosity satisfied by finally learning details of all that had taken place after Carl's rant?

Each December, as the holidays approached, Margo hoped this might be the year Angela would get in touch. Then, as one year bled into another, she came to accept their relationship was dead. When she looked back, as she was prone to do, she could see how her journey to acceptance had taken her through the cycles of grief. She'd gone down intermittent paths of denial, anger, hurt, bargaining and finally acceptance. She thought of the sign Angela bargained for in the antique shop all those years ago, "Friends – a Reason, a Season, a Lifetime." Angela had hung it over the doorway to her kitchen. Now, Margo imagined it gathering dust in the basement, or worse, tossed on some garbage heap.

Part Two

Chapter Thirteen

2012

M argo was in the kitchen making coffee. It was six thirty on a Monday morning in February of 2012. With an adrenalin rush, she ran and picked up the phone on the first ring, thinking, let it be a wrong number, there is no good news at this hour of the morning. "Hello?"

Silence, as though whoever was on the other end of the line was deciding whether to speak. "Hello?"

"Ma-argo?"

That voice? Angela? Could it be? So early in the morning? A sliver of hope emerged from that dark time of twelve years ago. Excitement rippled in her throat. The holidays were over. Had she thought of Margo the same way Margo had thought of her throughout December, when she gathered Christmas cards at the mailbox, hoping there would be one from Angela and Lou? Was she calling this early morning to follow through on a New Year's resolution to restore their friendship?

Despite the cascading thoughts regarding reconciliation, when she heard Angela's voice after all those years, an innate caution collided with expectation. "Is something wrong?"

Again, that hesitation Margo had always associated with Angela's unconscious deferral to Lou, before speaking her own mind. She could barely make out Angela's words when she whispered, "Lou died last night."

"What? Lou? Died? Last night?" Unable to take it in, she heard herself parrot the words back, more a question than a statement.

"Yes."

"Oh my God, no." Margo blurted, as she made her way to a chair, a straight-backed chair that would fortify her as she listened. The years streamed by on a river of the unspoken.

"What happened?"

Angela's response came in a rush of breathless phrases. "Lung cancer for a few months …out of the hospital… back at work… I went out to walk the dogs about five last night… came back …. disoriented…pulling things out of a closet… I called 911…hospital. The boys all came and while I was out of the room a doctor told them…your father is full of cancer. It was so quick."

"Oh Angela, I'm so sorry. I'm so glad you called me," as the realization struck, that after all these years, Margo was one of the first people Angela reached out to. Lou had passed away less than twenty-four hours ago. That told Margo something. She didn't know what it meant, but it was significant.

"I've missed you," Margo said.

"I know, I know. I don't know how it came to this."

"Well, no matter. We are talking now. Are the boys with you at the house now?"

"No, they went home and will be coming back in a little while. There's something else I must tell you…." again, the hesitation, "something worse."

"Something else? Worse?" What could be worse?

"It's Paul."

Margo waited. There was silence. Angela couldn't finish the sentence.

"Paul?"

"Paul died fifteen months ago."

Stunned, Margo couldn't believe what she was hearing. Angela came from a big Italian family. There were cousins named Paul and uncles named Paul; let it be an uncle, a cousin anyone but her firstborn.

"Not your Paul?"

"Yes."

The conversation seemed surreal. Margo heard herself gasp, unable to find words big enough to contain the enormity of what she was hearing. There were just the usual words. She heard herself repeating for the second time in a few minutes, "What happened?" an automatic question that follows all tragedy to buy some time in the effort to believe the unbelievable, to comprehend.

"It was a Friday, the day after Thanksgiving two years ago. Lou had told Paul at Thanksgiving dinner to take the day off. None of the family was working that day. But he had his own ideas. He went to work anyway and conceded to Lou by working only half a day." From these few words it sounded like Paul, who had consistently refused to work for his father, had reconsidered. This was a surprise to Margo, but now was not the time to ask a question. Angela continued, "He parked the car in his driveway around two. Lisa heard him pull in and when he didn't come into the house within a few minutes, she went outside to check. She found him slumped over the wheel. He was dead before the ambulance arrived. A heart attack."

"Oh Angela," was all she could utter, as her mind took in the reality. Her son, her firstborn had been gone from this earth for fifteen months and Margo hadn't known it. It seemed impossible. She thought of the two of them: twenty-three-year-old mothers pushing baby carriages along the tree-lined side-walks of Brooklyn, full of dreams for their babies' futures. The future was now. Paul, big like his father, but shy like his mother; Paul, the father of twin girls, the independent son who refused to be cajoled into the business. She thought of Declan, two months younger than Paul. Terror gripped her as she went to that place all mothers go, there but for the grace of God go I.

Margo's mind was a magnet latched onto Paul. She could not let go of his death, nor reach back to a few minutes earlier when she had registered Lou's death. She sensed Angela was caught in that transitional place too. How do you let go of one loss to give your full attention to the next? In the years that followed, she would learn from Angela that you don't.

Why didn't you let us know about Paul? The words itched behind Margo's tongue. Yet some instinct kept her from uttering them. They didn't matter compared to what Angela was telling her in the moment. The reality was, now she was telling her. Something had changed. That was enough. Lou had died a mere twelve hours ago, and this second death had somehow given her the freedom to speak to Margo about the first. The past twelve years evaporated. They had the rest of our lives to revisit the past.

They spoke for a long time. Mostly Angela talked and Margo listened as her old friend poured out her grief about trying to live without her dead son. It was as though she had to go in order, sequence the losses, revisit Paul's life and his death before she could enter the loss of the previous night. She talked for a long time about Paul. She mentioned things Margo had no way of knowing about, that had taken place during the years of their estrangement. His girls were both college students, he had sold his house and moved relatively near to her and Lou, and he had joined the business as Margo had surmised earlier in the call. This time she reacted, "In my memory, Paul was the holdout and refused to come on board at PARC."

"Oh, that changed years ago. It seems like he'd always had an office next to Lou's."

"Your four boys at PARC Labs. It must have been a dream come true for you and Lou," Margo said as she caught herself drifting into the past, picturing that same corner office, next to Lou's, where Finn once hung his skyline painting of New York City.

As they spoke, Margo felt their years of friendship reconstitute, word by word, the way millions of pixels on a tv screen sputter and coalesce into a whole picture. Death was constructing a bridge carrying them over the troubled waters of the past, yet the bridge to Lou had been forever washed away. For that Margo felt a renewed sorrow.

THE MORNING OF ANGELA'S CALL, ALARMED BY THE EARLY hour, Kevin got out of bed and came into the family room to see who Margo was talking to. He could tell from the seriousness of her tone that it was bad news and he mouthed, "Is it one of the kids?" the common question at the heart of a parent's worst nightmare. Somewhat relieved when she shook her head, he made his way into the kitchen and removed two mugs from the cabinet and filled the coffee pot. By the time the call ended, Kevin was hovering. He had gotten the drift of the conversation and he knew from hearing snippets of her end of the call that Lou was dead. She told him about Paul's death fifteen months prior.

"Oh, my God. And they never let us know. Why?"

Margo shook her head, baffled. "She doesn't know, or at least she offered no reason other than saying, 'I don't know how it came to this.'"

Later as they sat at the kitchen table with their coffee, the bright sun coming through the frosted windowpane was a counterpoint to Angela's grief. Snow had dusted every twig and branch in glistening white during the night. How could the world outside the window be so serene while death was happening. Margo's thoughts were a jumble. Balanced on the axis of her sorrow, a question spun. Why me? Why did she call me?

"Do you think the timing of Angela's call, just hours after Lou's death means it was Lou who engineered our separation for all those years?" she mumbled to Kevin.

Kevin had no answer. Neither of them wanted to believe that.

"Maybe she called in a semi-professional capacity because she is feeling desperate, and I am the only therapist she knows."

"Why would she do that?"

"She was a part of my life through all my training and early years of practice. I think she respected my career. Perhaps in a moment of despair in the hours after Lou died, she saw me as a therapeutic source more than a friend."

"Does the reason really matter?" Kevin asked.

He was right. Angela had called. That's what mattered. Still, she continued to wonder and a few minutes later, mused to Kevin, "I think she called because of our shared history. Regardless of how it ended, nothing can erase the closeness of the good years. They happened. They are part of all our lives."

Angela's telephone call was a pair of sturdy hands reaching out and pulling her through a hole in the ice, where their friendship had been submerged for years. She translated "Lou died last night," to "I want you back in my life." It wasn't the first time Margo considered it was Lou alone who had promoted the end of their friendship. What else could this reaching out imply? Although she couldn't imagine Lou forbidding Angela to make contact, she could see her deferring to his wishes, spoken or unspoken. Margo couldn't help wondering, if Lou had promoted the separation, what had prompted Angela to go against his wishes within hours of his death?

She stopped herself. What did it matter? They would go forward, not backwards.

Chapter Fourteen

2012

Two days later, snowflakes dusted the windshield and the roads threatened to freeze as Margo and Kevin made their way to Lou's wake. As Kevin maneuvered the car around a stalled truck he asked, "Did you order the floral arrangement?"

"Yes, it was to arrive this morning. I hope it's there before we get there."

"Why? What difference does it make when it arrives?"

Concerned that Angela's call might have been a momentary blip in her composure, that she could revert to whatever it was that had fueled the previous twelve years, Margo said, "I'm nervous about seeing Angela, nervous about seeing the family. The flowers arriving first will pave the way, make it less of a surprise to the three boys when we walk in. I'm especially nervous about seeing Carl. How about you? Are you nervous?"

"No, I'm just sad and full of regrets. I keep remembering all the good years. Somehow the last twelve years didn't feel final, more of an interruption, like a novel I put down but always knew I'd pick up again and finish. But Lou's dying is truly the end. There will be no finishing the story. In retrospect it all seems so small, doesn't it? So many wasted years."

When they entered the church's large foyer, the statue of the Virgin Mary, the banks of red and blue sanctuary candles, even the pamphlet rack on the wall, were much the same as they had been when they met them for Mass and dinner, that night in 2001. Margo heard Angela's familiar laugh before she saw her break away from visitors and rush towards them as they entered. She expected to find Angela wearing black, shaky, and unsteady, surrounded by her three sons. But no. She wore a dark green dress. Her hair was blonder than Margo remembered. She wore makeup.

"I'm so glad you're here" she said, as she kissed them, then grasped each of their hands tightly. She began introducing them to others waiting in the long line of mourners snaking through the foyer of the church and into the room where the casket lay.

"Margo and Kevin are our oldest, dearest friends. The four of us go way back to Brooklyn, before we were married," she said, as if Lou were standing there, completing their foursome, the way it had been when they travelled to Paris together.

Having talked to her two days earlier, Margo had glimpsed Angela's internal life. Now she was acting the role of hostess, greeting people, trying to make others comfortable. The boys and a hushed throng of visitors were all in an adjacent room where the casket stood, towards which the line was moving. The scent of flowers lining the walls spoke of death. A television screen in the corner, rotating photos of the family spoke of life. Margo watched the parade of photo's twice, curious to see if Kevin and she were included in this montage of family history. They were. There were two photos. The first was taken at Artie's baptism, the four of them so young as to be hardly recognizable, flanking the baby in Kevin's arms, the second, standing in front of the Eiffel tower in Paris. The inclusion of the photos spoke to Margo. They gave her a sense of having been pasted back into Angela and Lou's lives.

Angela stayed at their side, weaving them into conversation with the family, scattered in small groups within the hushed room. "You remember Lisa, Paul's wife." And of course, they did. They had been at her wedding twenty years earlier, and the christening of her twin girls, who stood on either side of her, looking pale and harried after their trips from their respective colleges. But as the past twenty-four hours had painfully revealed, she and Kevin had been absent from the most defining event of Lisa's life, her husband's funeral fifteen months earlier, which Margo imagined Lisa and her girls were reliving that very moment. Margo wondered if Lisa knew of the years of estrangement. She stifled the impulse to offer belated condolences as it became obvious, Lisa did not remember who they were. It wasn't important in that moment.

They continued to move through the room with Angela. "You remember Michelle?" she said, as they approached Artie's wife standing with one of her two children.

"Yes," Of course we do," Kevin said, as Michelle acknowledged their presence. Vague images of her wedding, the only wedding they had ever attended at a horse farm, flashed across Margo's mind. Michelle had a child from a previous marriage whom Artie had adopted, and they had since had another son, a five-year-old boy who was not present. Michelle was as Margo remembered her, outgoing and warm, and it was obvious she did remember them. As they passed Michelle, Angela whispered, "They're divorced. But at least they still talk to each other."

Margo didn't know how to respond. Angela absorbed her blank expression and continued, "Rob's wife, Rose, is another story. She's not here and not expected. They went through a messy divorce a few years ago. I'm waiting for her to drop off their two girls. I haven't seen them in months."

Two daughters-in-law gone through divorce. Grandchildren absent.

Images of Rose and Rob's elaborate Greek Orthodox wedding flashed before her. Handsome, well over six feet tall, with a head of black hair, Rob was a presence when he walked into a room, never more so than at his wedding, waiting at the altar in white tails, flanked by his brothers, as the organ boomed from high in the choir loft and his Rose walked down the massive aisle. Lou was in rare form that day, standing proudly on the cathedral steps greeting guests, and warning them about the three-hour ceremony, replete with candles and bells and incense and an abundant sprinkling of holy water in store for them. Angela had grabbed Margo's hand and nervously whispered, "See if you two can get him to quiet down, he's over-the-moon happy and making me crazy with his attempts to be funny."

From such an auspicious beginning, now Rob and Rose weren't speaking to each other, and Rose wasn't even expected at Lou's wake.

Angela continued to weave them through the crowded room towards her three sons flanking the casket. A flash of surprise registered on each of their faces when they saw their mother approaching with Margo and Kevin, as though a couple of ghosts had materialized from the past. Margo felt sure the boys didn't know Angela had reached out to them. Artie and Rob immediately extricated themselves from the group. They rushed towards them, arms extended and hugged them warmly. Carl remained where he was standing at the head of the casket.

"It's so good to see you here. How have you been? How's the family?"

"Fine, fine. So sorry," as they returned the hugs and mumbled condolences. After a few minutes, Artie and Rob returned to their positions alongside Carl.

Angela remained with them, clutching Margo's hand as they inched closer to the casket. She couldn't tell if Angela was trying to support her in this death ritual or if it were she who needed to feel Angela's skin on hers. Either way, Margo was grateful for her touch. The closer they got the more aware Margo became of being face to face with Carl. She had not made eye contact with him yet and sensed he was avoiding it, although it was likely Margo was holding back too. The fact that he hadn't spontaneously reached out with Artie and Rob seemed to imply there was something different between his brothers' reaction to unexpectedly seeing them and his. Probably guilt, Margo thought, as anxiety warned her the past was not as irrelevant as she wanted to believe.

There was a woman clinging to Carl's arm.

The casket was closed beneath a spray of white roses. Angela released Margo's hand and remained standing behind her and Kevin as they knelt in prayer. When they stood up, Angela reached towards the woman clinging to Carl,

"This is Eve, Carl's wife."

Meeting Carl's new wife, Margo felt conflicted. She had wanted to ignore the past, and yet ... Another milestone. There had been a fourth wedding during their estrangement. Within seconds, Carl extended his hand. They made eye contact. He showed no hint of discomfort or embarrassment. "Hello, thank you for coming." Margo's unanswered questions from 1998 rolled over her like fast-moving clouds. The old animosity, that for a few months had held her captive, stirred at the edge of consciousness. She felt it first in her sweaty palms, and the butterflies in her stomach. Did he remember? Did he feel awkward? Was she projecting her own awkwardness onto him? She was surprised at the flood of feelings seeing Carl brought up in her. She shook them off, like a dog with a flea.

As they moved on, Angela told them, "Eve is a cancer

survivor from many years ago. She recently had a scare. Carl is devoted to her. She is the love of his life."

Hearing how the weight of cancer was burdening Carl's marriage, softened the sharp edges of Margo's residual feelings towards him that had momentarily surfaced. The marriage was the brightest spot to emerge over the past decade for Angela. At least she had that.

"There's something inside the church I want you to see. Come"

She led them back through the lobby, still crowded with people, and into the church and pointed to a filigreed gold cross, suspended on chains, hanging from the dome above the altar. It must have been twelve feet in length, and it appeared to be floating in space.

"Lou and I had the cross commissioned in memory of Paul after he died."

They both gasped at its magnificence. "We were all here at the dedication ceremony when it was installed a few months ago. I wish so much you could have been with us. This is the only place in the world I get any comfort, Margo. I miss him so much," Angela whispered, as Margo observed a peace come over her as she raised her eyes to the cross.

Painfully aware that this was the first time in twelve years they had been together, Margo realized Angela needed to talk to her about Paul just as much as she needed to talk to Angela about all that led to this moment. He was the doorway through which they had to go, to enter this new death.

"You can't imagine what it's like, Margo. I see him everywhere. I dream him everywhere."

Memories cascaded from Angela's lips into the arid landscape of death. There was Paul, at birth, with that full head of black hair, the first born of all their children, Paul running in front of a car in Brooklyn, the screech of breaks, the ball rolling down the street, his innocent face as Lou scooped him up. Paul winning a track meet. Paul on the debate team. Paul organizing their twenty-fifth wedding anniversary party. Paul, the father of twins. Paul so alive. She was undoing his death in the telling, resurrecting her son for herself, for Margo. It wasn't until she got to his last hours: Paul pulling the car into the driveway, Paul failing to open the door, Lisa coming out the front door of the house to check on him, the ambulance, the end. This is when she lost her composure and the great gulping sobs came unbidden. It was as though Paul was dying all over again as the three of them sat beneath the cross in the empty church.

Eventually Angela gave them a sign that she was ready to return to the wake. They took seats alongside each other, in the straight-backed folding chairs set up in rows for mourners.

A little while later, Angela excused herself to greet someone, and her chair, which was between Kevin and Margo, became available. Artie must have been watching because within seconds he made his way over and sat down. He began talking earnestly to Kevin. Sensing a need for privacy, Margo excused herself and went to the lady's room. It wasn't until they were driving home that she asked Kevin,

"What was that all about with Artie?"

"Artie is an emotional mess."

"Well, they all are. It's understandable."

"No, this is more complicated. Artie told me he had a falling out with his father nine months ago and hadn't spoken to him since. Artie's left the business."

"He actually told you he left PARC Labs? I can't believe that."

"It's true. He's trying to start up his own business. He has been angry as hell at Lou. They evidently said some pretty awful things to each other, and now Artie knows he can never make it right."

"Did he tell you why he left?"

"He said he just couldn't work for his father anymore. Did

Angela say anything about that to you when you had that long talk on the phone the other morning?"

"No, not a word. Artie no longer with the business is still hard for me to take in. The dream of a family business goes back to the earliest days of their marriage. I can still remember them talking about it way back in Brooklyn, when the boys were babies."

"Me too. It must have killed Lou. It's killing Artie. He is really suffering. He asked me to meet with him next week. I gave him my phone number and I can only hope he calls, that reaching out today was not just an impulse that he will forget about tomorrow."

"Why do you think he chose you to confide in?"

"I don't know. I was as shocked as you are right now to learn that he left the business. But Lou and him not speaking to each other for almost a year? That shocked me even more."

"I can't imagine anything that would cause you to go so far as to cut off your relationship with one of our kids for even a day."

"Me either. Artie knows the history of Lou's and my relationship, how far back it goes, the estrangement, and his parents' long silence. Yet, here we are at his wake, as if all that never happened. I think maybe he felt I could relate to what it feels like to be a *persona non grata* to Lou."

Margo could only imagine what grief the trouble between Artie and Lou had brought into Angela's life that past year. Yet, in the hierarchy of losses, Angela didn't even mention it. Loss upon loss upon loss. It hadn't stopped for Angela.

Chapter Fifteen

2012

True to his word, Artie called Kevin the week after the funeral. They arranged to meet for lunch a few days later at a diner convenient to Artie's job.

Artie arrived before him. Unshaven, with dark circles under his eyes, he was seated at a corner table, a half-empty tumbler of scotch-on-the-rocks in front of him. Gone were the navy-blue suit and subdued gray tie he had worn at the wake, replaced by jeans, a faded tee shirt, and sneakers.

Kevin was taken aback. Artie looked like he had been wrestling with demons.

As he half arose from his chair to acknowledge Kevin's arrival, he took a big gulp of scotch. Kevin ordered coffee and felt a knife of memory in the pit of his stomach, for those days when alcohol was the main ingredient of his lunches too.

"How are you doing?"

"Not good."

"What's happening?"

"I can't focus on anything but my father. I keep asking myself why it had to end this way. I don't want to be angry with him. I can't believe I didn't speak to him for nine months before he died. But he didn't speak to me either."

"Yes. I get it. That is really unfortunate. What did you two argue about that it came to that?"

"Everything. We always argued but it really started to go downhill shortly after Finn left the company." In the disjointed conversation that followed, Kevin learned that while Finn was still at PARC Labs, Artie felt like he had a voice. Finn was an intermediary between him and his father. Finn listened to him, valued his ideas, and implemented them. He felt they were all building something new, going someplace. "It was exciting, and I liked going to work."

After Finn left, it became harder and harder for him to work there. He'd put in over twenty years, never worked anyplace else since graduating from college. He wanted to leave but couldn't bring himself to do it. He started to drink, and his marriage fell apart. At this point, he picked up his glass of scotch and raised it, as if to toast his defeat. "There were times I wanted to call Finn and get his advice about starting my own thing, but I knew my father would see that as a betrayal. So, I never did. I hung in there, year after year, for another ten years, until 2010."

"That's a lot of years," Kevin said as he absorbed the history of PARC in which Artie was caught. "What changed in 2010?"

He took a deep breath, and another gulp of scotch, and signaled the waitress for a refill. "That's when my brother Paul died. One minute he was fine, the next he was dead. I'm only a year younger than Paul. I was scared. Life is short, too short to be miserable every day. I knew if I didn't do it then, I'd never leave." Artie's hands trembled holding the empty glass.

"'I told my father I wanted to cash in my shares of PARC and use the money to start my own company,"

It wasn't hard for Kevin to conjure Lou's reaction. "I

suspect that didn't go well. I know from the time you and your brothers were babies he wanted all you boys in the business with him."

"You've got that right," Artie said loudly, causing customers at the next table to glance their way, "In the beginning we had reasonable talks. He and my mother both tried to talk me out of leaving. When I kept insisting, things got ugly with my dad. He deliberately undervalued my shares. It was money I'd earned. I had a right to the cash," he said as he pulled a handkerchief from his pocket and wiped the beads of perspiration that had started to form on his forehead. Getting more agitated as he talked, he explained he was determined to create a business as successful as PARC Labs and prove to his father that he could do it on his own. "I wanted to show him the side of me he'd never bothered to see for himself. I told him I'd hire a lawyer and sue him for what was rightfully mine. He told me to go ahead and get an attorney. He assured me I'd lose. I thought once I brought an attorney into it, he would be embarrassed, shamed, and it would force him to do the right thing."

"And?"

"My father went ahead and hired his own attorney to help him cheat me. My mother tried to talk him out of it. She knew I had to get away, but my father wouldn't listen to her. Just shut her down."

In the end, Artie got just a small percentage of what his shares were worth. "My own father screwed me," he said, as he banged his palm on the table, and his anguish echoed across the restaurant. "That was the last day I spoke to him. Now it's too late. I'll never be able to make it right." Tears started to roll down his cheeks as he stood up and mumbled he was going to the rest room.

Kevin's heart ached for Artie as he watched him walk across the room. He saw, underneath the hulking shoulders, a little boy searching for his father. As he sat at the table, waiting for

Artie to return, his mind raced with thoughts about how to help. He asked himself, why would Lou do that, cheat his own son? Yet he couldn't know for sure that Lou undervalued the stock. Lou wasn't here to tell his side of the story. Perhaps it was a ploy to get Artie to give up on the idea of leaving and starting his own company? More likely Lou thought he would squander the money. Drink it away. Artie had told him earlier that he started to drink when his marriage fell apart. Seeing him with that half-empty glass of scotch at eleven this morning… Perhaps Lou just wanted to keep him in the fold where he could keep an eye on him and influence his behavior.

Kevin also wondered if Artie knew about his own drinking problem in the eighties. How he had been helped by AA. Artie would have been only seventeen or eighteen at that time and Kevin knew from raising his own family, kids at that age are hardly interested in anything outside their own lives. Yet, Artie may have had some inkling. Especially if Lou or Angela had used what they knew about Kevin's loss of his business and eventual rehab as a cautionary tale with their son. If that was the case, perhaps it was the reason Artie approached him at the wake and asked to meet. He was still sorting out his thoughts when Artie returned to the table. He was calmer. He had washed his face and straightened his football-player shoulders under his rumpled shirt. After he sat down, he looked Kevin in the eye and said, "Can I ask you a question?"

"Of course."

Kevin thought he was going to ask him for help with his drinking. But it wasn't that at all. Wiping his forehead, where beads of perspiration had erupted, he asked, "Did my father ever talk to you about my leaving the business or our fight and lawsuit?"

The question was the last thing Kevin was expecting. He hedged by asking, "What makes you think he talked to me about you?"

"When I saw you with my mother at the funeral...she was holding on to your hand... I didn't know you were in contact ... I thought ... I hoped maybe my father and you had started talking again too ... and that I just wasn't aware of it ... and maybe he talked to you about me?"

Kevin suddenly understood. The urgent need for this meeting had been Artie's *Hail Mary* prayer to uncover any shred of evidence that his father had confided to someone, anyone, a desire to mend his relationship with his son.

Taken aback, Kevin had no choice but to admit the truth. He watched the disappointment register on Artie's face as he told him, "No, I haven't talked to your father in over ten years, but I wish he had come to me. I would have told him to make it right with you. I'm sure your rift was hurting him as much as it was hurting you."

"I doubt that" Artie said sarcastically.

Speaking as the father of three children, Kevin suggested that it was possible Lou thought he wasn't ready to go it alone; that Artie still needed him. "He may have tried to make it hard for you to leave, perhaps as a way of protecting you," That doesn't mean he was right. But I can tell you, you don't stop loving your son just because you're angry with him."

Artie started to tear up. "I made a few mistakes when I was a teen-ager and he never trusted me after that. He pretended he did, but I knew he was always expecting me to mess up. I proved him right. I really am messed up now."

"There were things about your father I didn't understand either," Kevin confessed. "I was baffled about why our friendship came to a halt after Finn left. I wondered if he was angry with me and Margo for not interceding and talking Finn out of leaving."

Artie shook his head in a gesture of helplessness as he once again beckoned the waitress. "Who knows? My father held grudges. He didn't talk to his own father for years for who knows what reason. He stopped talking to his younger brother when he got divorced and remarried. Stupid stuff. It was my mother who kept in touch with my uncle. My father's own brother was dead to him."

"That explains a lot. It wasn't just me and Margo who were shut out?'

"No, I think he thought Finn was eventually going to see things his way and took it personally when Finn resigned. My father didn't like anyone to walk away from him. He liked to be in control."

"He must have known Finn was unhappy," Kevin said, "with Lou's unilateral decision to sell Bakers Palette and how that changed the original business plan."

"I certainly knew Finn was unhappy," Artie said. "Rob knew too. We talked to my father, both together and separately about the decision, and the whole Christmas Eve incident and all it indicated. When he thought he was right that's the way it was going to be. The end. There was no getting him to budge."

THAT EVENING, MARGO DROPPED INTO A CHAIR ACROSS FROM Kevin, her coat still on. She kicked off her shoes as she placed her briefcase and purse alongside the chair. It was nine. She'd just gotten home from seeing her evening clients. She was anxious to hear about the meeting.

"How did it go today?"

Kevin turned off the football game he was watching, a sign that this would be a long and serious conversation. He sighed and said, "I'm not sure," as he began to recount the lunch with Artie.

As she absorbed everything Kevin was telling her, the clock on the mantle chimed eleven. She still had her coat on her lap and as she maneuvered out of the chair, she thought of a client she had seen that very evening. The young woman revealed her emancipated status, granted by a court, from her parents. It had been a wrenching action taken by the girl and her three younger siblings to escape the emotional abuse of mentally compromised parents. In its aftermath, she had enough insight to seek therapy. Her parents did not. They lived in their bubble of righteousness. Like Lou. The situations were different but the potential for devastation was endless.

Kevin started to stack the days newspapers, scattered around his chair, as if to indicate he had told her everything. Then, almost as an afterthought, he began again. "One more thing. Artie told me something that let me know Finn's leaving wasn't the end of the story for Lou."

"How so?"

"One day he walked into Lou's office and glimpsed a head-line on his screen about the merger of Cordelia and Bogard. Lou quickly shut down the computer. Artie thought no more of it until weeks later when he learned that Finn had managed the merger and realized his father was still tracking Finn's career."

"Wow," Margo said, as she thought of that night at Lunello, when she so wanted to tell Lou about Finn's success, and he preempted her with news about their new apartment in Manhattan. "Lou knew all along!"

"It seems so." Artie speculated the more successful Finn was the more Lou resented his leaving. "He just didn't allow himself to be in a position where he would be reminded of someone else's success. He couldn't handle that."

"Being Lou's son wasn't easy. Being his wife wasn't easy either."

"Why do you say that?"

"Artie asked me if Angela called us when Paul died and when I told him she hadn't, Artie just shook his head ruefully. He told me his mother wanted to notify us but 'with my father, who knows?' He seemed to imply that Lou dissuaded her."

"I can only imagine what they all went through," Margo

161

said, as the same icy fear associated with any child's death crawled up her spine.

"How did you leave it with Artie? Will you see him again?"

"Yes. We talked a bit about his drinking after he brought it up. I offered to meet again or go to some AA meetings with him when and if he is ever ready. His choice. He seemed grateful. I told him how much AA had helped me when I was struggling. We're going to meet again next week."

When the following week rolled around, Artie called and cancelled. They rescheduled for the subsequent week. He cancelled again. And again. Soon Artie stopped returning Kevin's calls.

Chapter Sixteen

2013

The scab of betrayal and hurt that had grown over Margo's affection for Lou and Angela was loosened by his death. She was flooded with thoughts of all they had lost in those twelve years. Other friendships had come and gone, some ebbed and flowed on the tides of circumstance, others remained steadfast. None had ended so purposefully and so completely as with Lou and Angela.

She didn't want them to drift apart again, wary that some loyalty to Lou might surface, causing Angela to pull back, regret reaching out. She thought of what elevates a stranger to an acquaintance, to a friend. Random conditions as diverse as the neighborhood you live in, the school you attend, the classmate at the next desk, the church you find yourself frequenting, the co-worker, the teammate, any one of hundreds of shared interests or experiences can draw one to another. Even the unlikelihood of a blizzard that shuts down the city for a day. Every friend was once a stranger that some alchemy of personality or proximity nursed into something more. Like snowflakes, no two friendships are exactly alike. The events of the previous weeks had compelled Margo to look back at the various friend-ships in her life. Few had made the leap from the reason or the season, to become a lifetime friendship. For Margo, that was the gold standard. Like those antique treasures they collected, while pushing baby carriages in Brooklyn all those years ago, the value of friendship increased with how long it endured. Over time she and Angela had discovered connections to each other that validated, supplemented, and enhanced what was important to them, what was worth the effort to keep the friendship alive. Until it wasn't.

As they stood in line at Lou's funeral, hadn't Angela intro-duced them as "our oldest dearest friends from before we were married?" She wondered if there was any language that had distinct words to capture the various kinds of friendships. A word to encompass the variation that makes one friendship different from another, one word that tells of the unique experi-ence behind the reason, the season, the lifetime, like the one hundred words the Inuit of Alaska use to describe their experi-ences of snow.

With Lou's death and Angela's call, Margo reframed their friendship as *lifetime with interruption.* The moment they walked into Lou's wake and Angela hastened to them, as though it had been twelve days not twelve years since they'd last seen each other, her foreboding evaporated. Something rekindled within her. It would be different. There would be three of them, no longer a foursome. But where there had been nothing for twelve years, now there was something.

Determined to be the best friend she could, Margo called Angela frequently. These phone calls would be their new geog-raphy. There were many times Angela was too distraught to pick up the phone and just let it ring. Often, Margo could sense her wanting to cut the call short, get back to her bed, where her dog stationed himself, like a sentry, on the floor alongside her. Margo's heart wrenched when Angela confided, "Women from

St. Augustine's stop by with bagels or casseroles, but I don't want to see anyone. I tell them to leave the food in the garage."

On the days she was able to engage, they talked about Paul, and they talked about Lou. Angela continued to need to revisit her son's death before she could move on to Lou's death or anything else. Bit by bit, Margo learned that during the years they were estranged, their social life continued to revolve around St. Augustine's and the weekend apartment they'd purchased on 86th Street in Manhattan. Visiting museums and galleries, attending Broadway shows, and discovering new restaurants filled their weekends. After Paul's death that stopped. Now Angela was determined to sell the apartment.

"There's nothing there for me without Lou. He did all the planning, I just followed along."

If they weren't in the city, Angela explained, each Saturday evening they made their way to Mass at St. Augustine's. Afterwards, they joined a few couples for dinner. With Lou dead, she removed herself from the group. "I'm a woman alone now, no one wants me tagging along." she added bitterly.

Margo tried to challenge her thinking, giving her examples of Kevin and her continuing relationships with their widowed friends. "It's different here," Angela said dismissively. "Maybe if we had taken up tennis like you and Kevin or joined the Italian American Club or even learned to play bridge, there would be more friends to rely on. The business and the family took up all our time."

The extended family included a bevy of cousins and nieces and nephews, all from Angela's side, but they were geographically scattered, many still in Brooklyn, others on Long Island.

Angela's biggest source of support was Father Rich, the pastor at St. Augustine's. It was Father Rich who counselled them through Paul's death, and it was Father Rich to whom she continued to turn. He would pray with her and for a few minutes her despair would lift. Yet once she left his little office in the rectory, her grief would once again consume her. After about six months, Margo tentatively asked "Have you ever thought of going to a grief group?"

"I don't know how that would help. I go see Father Rich and he's trying to help me."

"Maybe you will feel less alone with people who are going through the same thing."

"Where would I even find one?"

"I'll help you."

"Maybe, I'll let you know."

She didn't take Margo up on the offer, but when Father Rich suggested it to her a few weeks later, she went reluctantly.

"I'm not going back," she told Margo after a few meetings. "Listening to others doesn't help me. It makes me feel worse. No one there has lost a son and a husband."

After a few months, she forced herself to go into the office a few times a week. Leaving her bed, getting dressed, driving to the office and being with the staff, who had genuine affection for her, gave her week some structure. Mostly it gave her an opportunity to see the boys.

When Angela spoke of PARC Labs, the implication was always that the three boys still worked there. Although Margo knew Artie had left the business, it cost her nothing to respect the secret Angela needed to maintain and pretend otherwise. She never brought up the lawsuit and rift between Artie and Lou. She doubted Angela even knew Artie had reached out to Kevin at the funeral. Margo didn't see this as an overt lie, just an omission. She went along. In the hierarchy of loss Angela endured, this one remained unspeakable for Angela.

Margo understood. In many ways she was not much different. There were subjects Kevin and she had not been forthcoming about either. Hadn't they kept the tumultuous years of alcohol dependance a secret until Kevin was in recovery? It was one thing to speak with your own family about difficult issues, but it felt like betrayal to acknowledge shame and failure with someone outside the family. It is only in retrospect that Margo could see a pattern that had gradually developed over the years, one of avoidance and secrets. They all played their part in following some unspoken rule. It must have served them well because they never changed it. Most likely, inherited from their families, it was unspoken and binding—don't air your dirty laundry in public. Just what constituted "dirty laundry" was amorphous. Anything that caused you or your family to appear less than bright and shiny was best kept under wraps, like a silver coin that would tarnish if exposed to the air. It was only when a crisis was under control that they were able to reveal it.

There was one night at Lunello when Lou, his tongue loosened by the red wine, had turned to Angela, and said, "Well, shall we tell them?"

"Tell them what?"

"About almost going bankrupt."

"What?" Lou had their attention. He never talked about a business problem, no less something as major as going bankrupt. However, the laugh and sly smile that accompanied the announcement, as he reached for the basket of bread, broke the tension, and gave a hint. He was about to reframe some bad experience into something absurd. Transform what could have been a tragedy into comedy. Margo glanced at Angela with an inquisitive look. She wasn't laughing, but she didn't seem upset either. As usual, she deferred to Lou.

"Last year Artie took off for Las Vegas after a night of drinking and married some co-ed he met at a party."

"Married?"

"Yes. I send him to college and give him a job with the world at his feet and he gets plane tickets and a four-dollar marriage certificate. When he finally sobered up and I hammered a little sense into him, it was up to me to finance an annulment with the church and divorce from the co-ed."

167

Lou had the marriage undone and paid the young woman enough to ensure she would never be heard from again. One more incident to add to Lou's personal log of saving-the-day stories in the family archives. Once again, Margo and Kevin glimpsed the sorrow of the previous months through the refracted lens of its having been relegated to the past. How upsetting it might have been was erased by its resolution.

Some things were acceptable to share, events over which you had no control, like the death of a parent, a child having trouble in school, a miscarriage or broken leg, a flooded basement, events the world thrust on you. But events tinged with deep personal shame, or a sense of inadequacy or failure, like Kevin's drinking and the loss of the business, remained unspoken between them, until after they'd been resolved. Or never told. Margo suspected that Artie's blow-up with his father was carved into Angela's heart where it would remain forever buried in the vault of the never told.

This need to be private was probably part of the symmetry that drew Margo and Angela together all those years ago. Being sensitive to perceived boundaries allowed them to curate what they revealed about their marriages, their families, and their failures. As much as Margo wanted to satisfy her curiosity about what was behind that Christmas Eve meeting, her long-ingrained sense of overstepping a boundary prevailed. This, despite her years as a psychotherapist, when time after time, she witnessed healing take place, sentence by sentence, once the wall of silence was broken. Her father too, in his concrete way, had taught her the value of probing beneath the surface. Still, she fell into the old patterns.

SHE WAS THIRTEEN YEARS OLD WHEN, ONE SATURDAY MORNING, her father awakened her to ask if she would help him salvage a round, forty-year-old tiger oak pedestal table from Nathan's Bar

& Grill in Brooklyn. Nathan and his wife were closing the neighborhood tavern after thirty years of serving draft beer and hot dogs. He had saved the biggest table for her father.

That May morning, her father lay on his back in the sawdust covering the barroom floor and unscrewed the hardware holding the table together. Margo held the flashlight, all the while taking in the abuse the table had endured. It was sticky from years of Rheingold spilling froth over the rims of glasses. Someone had sketched a stem and petals onto three inkblots staining the wood, disguising them as a bouquet of daisies. Chewing gum hung like boils to the underside of the edges. A crooked heart with four fragile initials was carved into the apron and hundreds of black rings from sweating pilsner glasses overlapped the scarred wood where ashes from cigarettes pocked the surface.

They carted it piece by piece through the early morning streets of Brooklyn, pausing occasionally to reposition their slipping fingers or to share the story of their bounty with a neighbor, before lugging the last of it through the cellar door and into her father's workroom.

Each night after dinner her father disappeared into the basement to work on the table. First, he stripped the varnish with application after application of Red Devil paint remover. Sometimes Margo helped. She watched it bubble up like silt in a pond after rain. The layers of varnish and misuse turned into a thick pasty liquid they peeled off with their scrapers until the intricate grain of the golden oak reappeared. They sanded it by hand. First with sandpaper number nine, the roughest paper needed to remove the deepest scars, and finally with sandpaper number one for a delicate finish. The air was thick with dust that made its way up the stairs and passed through small cracks around the door and into the kitchen. Her mother protested. Still, they kept on sanding, oblivious to the dust that was, in retrospect, risky business.

"Always sand with the grain, never against," her father said. "Be patient," he urged as he rubbed his hand over the gleaming surface. They were midwives ministering to the holy moment when the grain in the wood floated to the surface as if from underwater. "Just look at that," he said as he admired their work. "Who would believe that something so beautiful was hidden under all the goop."

They worked side-by-side under the naked bulb hanging from the basement ceiling socket. While the metal hardware soaked in Red Devil, they bathed the newly sanded wood with turpentine, applied varnish, waited twenty-four hours for it to dry, and then buffed it with the finest steel wool. "Be patient," he counseled again as Margo's thirteen-year-old self showed signs of wanting to skip a few steps. Finally, it was finished. Reassembled.

For years it has had a place in her office, an office where others trust her with their stories. She listens as layers of hurt, shame, anger, regret, and sorrow are loosened, then bubble to the surface. Together, she and her clients scrape away the toxic brew. This is when she hears the echo of her father's voice, "Could you believe something so beautiful was hidden under all that goop." He called her to witness those moments, which never fail to emerge, when the truth at the core of every person's story is revealed, and both speaker and listener are transformed.

Yet she could not get to that place of peeling back the layers with Angela. It would take years before an unguarded moment arose and she was finally able to leap over her self-imposed boundary.

Chapter Seventeen

2013

Other than her dog, Teeter, who was the loadstone of her grief, there seemed to be one reliable bright spot in Angela's life, Carl's happiness in his marriage. It was the week of Carl and Eve's anniversary when Angela surprised Margo by mentioning their wedding. It was the only wedding of all their children that the four of them had not witnessed together.

"I'd given up on his ever getting married. I wish you and Kevin had been there."

"Me too."

They seemed to be approaching the doorway to a conversation Margo had been longing to have, a conversation about Carl. Each time his name came up, the urge to ask what happened with him and Finn rushed on some river of adrenalin into her brain. She would think, maybe today? Butterflies fluttered in the pit of her stomach, her palms dampened with anxiety as she asked herself, what are you going to do with the information? Will you take some satisfaction in an admission of wrongdoing towards Finn? Does Angela even know what happened? For a moment the words trembled on her tongue, then, one by one, disassembled. Like remnants of stars consumed by a black hole, they did not escape the forces holding them within her. That would take another five years.

Angela, a lilt in her voice, continued, "Like everything with Carl and Eve, it's a quirky story." She laughed, for the first time in months. Carl was forty-one when they met at a county fair in Frenchtown, both admiring handmade quilts and bantering with the Amish woman who designed and created them. They were interested in the same quilt; Eve couldn't afford it and Carl could. This woman, who they have since come to refer to as "the matchmaker" was trying to make a sale. She peered at Carl from behind the wall of quilts hanging in her little booth and said, "Why don't you buy it and have the young lady over for a visit to see it again." Carl was smitten; he bought the quilt and gave it to Eve on the spot.

A flash of warmth infused Margo's opinion of Carl as she listened.

"They were made for each other, with their county fairs, and all cotton clothes. Neither of them will go near a nylon or polyester thread," Angela said, in a rare moment of light-heartedness. They were married seven short months later, in 2006, six years before Lou died. Margo did a quick calculation. That would have been six years after Finn left PARC Labs.

"It sounds like you really like her."

"She's different. Ten years younger than Carl and not easy to get close to. She has some awkward ways about her.

"Awkward? How so?"

"You know how my family loves the Fourth of July holiday? One year Eve shocked us by offering to host it." Angela started to laugh explaining how the couple served their Italian family tofu and bean sprouts at the dining room table while the rest of the country was sitting under the stars with hamburgers and hot dogs. "Lou and I stopped at a diner on the way home."

"You told me at the wake that Eve was a cancer survivor.

Do you think that has anything to do with her unconventional ways?"

"I don't know. They say she is completely cured, but I know they both worry."

"What kind of cancer did she have?"

"I'm not sure. It's all kind of vague. I've learned not to pry. Eve keeps to herself. They like to be alone, and from the beginning, it's been hard to get them to visit. She refuses to learn to drive. Carl drives her everywhere. But I'm used to it now. I get to see Carl during the week at work. Truth be told, without Eve around, it's easier to talk to him."

"Their old Victorian house is their baby, the baby they will probably never have," she said mysteriously. "It means everything to them, and they've worked hard to fix it up. It was featured on a house tour and was showcased in the local newspapers for the way they restored it."

"Sounds like quite a house."

"Yes, but it would be nice to be allowed in it with your shoes on. She keeps slippers by the front door and it's either that or stocking feet. "

"Well, these days that's what people do."

"I guess ... Lou asked her once if she wanted him to buy velvet ropes for the rooms we're not allowed in. She didn't think it was funny."

There seemed to be a vulnerability and innocence about Eve that charmed Carl, if not Angela, as taking care of his wife became the vocation of his happiness. Although Angela found Eve odd, Carl's contentment more than compensated for putting up with her eccentricities.

During those calls they talked about the piano lessons Lou never had time for, the now aborted plans for enlarging the deck off the kitchen, the pending sale of the apartment in New York, Christmas Eve that would no longer be celebrated with Lou's seven courses of fish, the Sunday dinner table, empty, one Sunday after another. In that first year, Angela confided one other bright note in her grieving life. Rob had started dating a nurse, Diana, whom he met at the hospital when Lou was dying. He was moving on from his divorce. Carl's marriage, Rob's finding Diana, Father Rich, and her dog were the life rafts that kept her afloat.

As the months went by, they talked about Margo's life too, her work as a psychotherapist, Kevin, the family, Margo's sisters, whom Angela knew slightly from the Brooklyn days. A part of her wanted to speak freely, as she did about Maura and Declan, but it seemed impossible to talk about how Finn's life evolved without referencing his departure from PARC Labs. It still felt like a taboo subject.

Margo had the peace of knowing Finn had righted his life, moved on, to the extent that his experience at PARC Labs was no more than a faded memory to him. Angela never asked, and Margo never offered more details of Finn's life. They talked around him as though he were a stick-figure in the background of a family portrait.

"What's it like living in a condo?" Angela asked during one of their many phone conversations. "Do you miss the old house and all the memories?" Margo thought the question might indicate a shift in Angela's thinking, a loosening in her determination to stay in the house where she and Lou had launched the business and their children. It held all the memories she clung to.

"Why don't you come for a visit? I can show you around and tell you all about condo living. I love it."

"No, I'm not ready to travel."

Margo persisted and finally, after a few aborted dates, it happened. Angela hired a driver for the afternoon and when she arrived, she seemed proud of herself. "I can't believe I did it. I'm here, Ta da." For an hour or so they were the old Angela and Margo, reminiscing about floor plans and color schemes and especially Eugenia Shepherd's School for Brides. As Angela looked at the wall of bookcases surrounding the fireplace, an impish grin erupted on her face,

"Do you remember the bookcases we built in our first apartments?"

"Oh my God, what a fiasco that was," Margo said, as the memory took shape in her mind. They started to giggle. In their search for affordable decorating ideas, they had stumbled upon a way to construct a bookcase and decorate the books to match the room. The four of them went to a lumber yard and purchased six-foot-long planks of pine. They stained the planks walnut, stacked bricks in two columns and inserted the planks, creating three shelves. The big mistake was pasting colored stick-on crepe paper, to match the colors of the furniture, along the spine of each book. Lime green and deep purple for Margo and Kevin. Red and black for Angela and Lou. Margo confessed to Angela, "I still have books with blotches of glue staining their spines from when I removed the colored crepe paper so we could make out the titles and authors."

"Me too!" Angela said. "There was a book by Graham Green that Lou liked to reread occasionally. I'd glued red paper over the spine and binding. A year later he was looking for it. It took him going through every book on those shelves to find it. He was not happy. I still have that glue-stained copy saved with his Graham Green collection." By now they were laughing like teen-agers, revisiting a treasured memory pulled from the dustbin of history.

When Kevin came home from work, surprising Angela, she started to cry. "I wish it was the four of us."

"I know," Kevin answered, giving her a hug.

Margo left Angela and Kevin alone and went into the kitchen to fuss over coffee and scoop ice cream into bowls. She was half listening to the chatter in the other room when she heard Angela say, "Artie left the family business and started his own operation. He's now living in Pennsylvania."

Kevin feigned surprise. "Is it the same kind of business as PARC Labs?"

"More or less." He wanted to build something for himself. Prove to himself he could do it. And he has. I'm so proud of him."

Kevin listened. He didn't let on that Artie had told him about the blow-up and lawsuit with his father. He didn't share he had subsequently met with Artie and tried to mend his brokenness. Angela had evidently made peace with that part of the past. It was good news to learn Artie had landed on his feet. Kevin would tell Finn. He knew Finn always had faith in Artie.

Later, after they'd consumed the last swirls of ice cream, Angela said to Kevin,

"I was going through some old photographs recently and found a Polaroid of you and Lou taken that day of the blizzard in 1959. I brought it with me." She got up and collected her purse from where she had left it, alongside a chair in the living room. She retrieved the faded photo and the three of them put their heads together to look at it. It was an opportunity to revisit the past. Margo hoped Angela might say something to Kevin about Lou, some words to bridge that twelve-year gully that they all ignored, something revealing like, "Lou always regretted ... or Lou was going to call you so many times ..." But that didn't happen. She realized Angela no longer felt the gap, felt the need for the bridge. It was as though, to her, the friendship reestablished between the three of them had reintegrated Lou, and the twelve-year estrangement had never happened.

All in all, it was a good day, sprinkled with bright moments when Angela seemed to return to herself in the few months allotted her before it all came crashing down again.

Chapter Eighteen

2014

Kevin and Margo carted two huge pumpkins from the car and placed them on the kitchen table. It was a late Sunday afternoon in October of 2014. Returning from an afternoon of pumpkin-picking, topped off by a hayride with Maura and her twins, they were happily exhausted. The red light on the answering machine was blinking annoyingly as Kevin went to retrieve the calls before taking his jacket off. They listened to a one sentence recorded message, "This is Artie Romano, call me back on my mobile phone as soon as you pick up this call." They looked at each other, surprised. It had been a year and a half since a troubled Artie poured out his grief to Kevin. The message sounded ominous.

"I hope nothing is wrong with Angela," Margo said, somewhat alarmed by the cryptic message. "I spoke with her a few days ago, but you never know with Angela, she is so private."

Kevin, on the other hand, stayed calm, "I think it's more likely he is following up on my offer to help him after the funeral." After hanging up his jacket and grabbing a bottle of water, Kevin dialed the phone. Margo watched from across the then as his face went pale, seconds after saying hello. She heard him repeat "An accident?" He listened. "Oh God, how awful."

Margo thought for sure Angela had died. Then she heard Kevin say,

"How's your mother?" Fear, coiled in her chest like a spring, began to unwind.

It wasn't Angela. The call was short. Kevin didn't ask for details. They didn't matter. No detail of fate or timing could change what he'd just learned. As he hung up the phone, he turned towards Margo and said, "Carl was killed in an automobile accident on a back-country road as he drove home from work on Friday."

The mind rejects the reality, but the heart knows better and trembles at its core. This could not be happening to Angela again. Weak kneed by the news, Margo wondered out loud to Kevin, what could possibly have caused a fatal accident on a country road on a beautiful autumn afternoon? Her mind flew to drinking and alighted on Friday afternoon happy hour. Artie had told Kevin about his drinking problem. There's a genetic component to alcoholism. Brothers with the same genes. She thought of the many nights she'd worried about Declan, Maura, or Finn, when as teen-agers they were late getting home from a date or a party, fearing their father's genes would manifest in one of them.

"Was it alcohol?"

"I don't know."

Margo immediately censored herself for faulting Carl. She asked herself if some residual blame she had placed on him for his part in attempting to torpedo Finn's career, was slithering from her subconscious, like a snake from under a rock? There were a few months in 1999 when she was so angry with him, she wanted retribution, pay back for the hurt he had inflicted. A vague desire for justice had come unbidden to her thoughts, some version of an eye-for-an-eye, a tooth-for-a-tooth. Bu this, Oh God, not this.

A reel of years unspooled in her mind. Carl at ten years old. A shy boy, crying. Lou picking him up off the ice on the pond in Princeton, stopping the game while the other kids complained. Lou, passing him the puck so he could shoot for a goal. Carl, with his odd Eve whom he adored. Carl, the grim young architect Finn had described, who walked around the factory in Barney's fashions. The ghost of an amorphous guilt, for having wanted retribution, materialized from the ether. She found herself staring into the ugliest part of her soul. Shame gnawed at her. It metamorphosized into an intense desire to undo the tragedy, to reverse time to the minutes before the accident, give Angela her son back, give Artie and Rob their brother back, give Carl his life back.

Carl was the same age as Paul when he had a fatal heart attack on that November day six years before. Angela's oldest and youngest sons. Both gone. Who knows what sinister fate lurks in the genes of children, waiting to undo their lives? She thought of her own children. The randomness of tragedy. The aftershock rocked her.

She turned to God. Always her default; another element of symmetry she shared with Angela. She prayed for Carl with the same intensity she had faulted him. Angela was living the worst tragedy Margo could conjure. Margo argued with God. Although the laws of the universe make no promises, we rely on them to keep a certain order. We count on them to keep our children alive beyond our own deaths. If it could happen to Angela, it could happen to anyone, it could happen to her. Where was God in all this, the keeper of the laws of the universe?

ONCE AGAIN, THEY DROVE TO ST. AUGUSTINE'S FOR A WAKE AND funeral. Another closed casket. Another flower-laden room. Eve, pale and shaken, stood alongside the coffin, flanked by her mother and two sisters. They appeared to be guarding her, wary of anyone getting too close. It was understandable. She looked to be in shock.

Angela too was dazed. Sedated. Seated between Artie and Rob, she didn't seem to be aware of the mourners coming and going around her. Father Rich hovered behind her chair. As Margo bent down to speak to her, Angela looked up. She grabbed both of Margo's hands and clung to them. Her eyes were the saddest eyes she'd ever seen. "What am I going to do? What am I going to do?" she asked over and over. Margo had no answer. No one had an answer.

Kevin and Margo took a seat in the eerily silent room. A few minutes later, Artie left Angela's side and made his way to them. He looked good. Clean shaven, dressed in a business suit. He had gained some weight which made him look so much like Lou that Margo's breath caught in her throat as he approached. He sat in an adjacent chair. He seemed to have taken on the mantle of representing the family. "We don't know what happened," he said, even before asked. "There was an autopsy, but we don't have the results yet."

The police suspected it was a medical incident. The preliminary investigation indicated there was no mobile phone or alcohol involvement. An investigation determined Carl was driving west on his way home from work around four-thirty. His car collided into the east bound lane, hitting a Honda Accord driven by a thirty-nine-year-old woman, also on her way home from work. Her car struck the guardrail on the side of the road. Carl's Porsche came to a stop in the middle of the road. "That's where the police found them," Artie concluded.

"Did anyone witness what happened?"

"No. A driver came upon the accident right after it happened and called it in. But he didn't witness it."

"The other driver. What happened to the woman?"

"The medics attempted to revive her, but she was pronounced dead at the scene. They flew Carl to a trauma center, but he was dead before they got there."

"Do you think he had a heart attack, like Paul?"

"We don't know what to think. He was fine when he left the office. No medical issues. He took care of himself. Went for his yearly check-ups. We just don't know." With that, he stood up," I want to get back to mom." Before he turned to go, he looked Margo directly in the eyes and said, "Stay in touch with my mother. She needs a friend."

It took a few weeks before Angela was able to talk about what happened. At the wake and funeral, she was mostly mute. Now she needed to speak about this final day in her son's life from the beginning, including the hours before the accident, the sacred minutes when Carl was not dead.

"It was like any other Friday," she explained. "He always stopped by my desk and teased me about what kind of cookies he wanted me to bake for the following week. Half the time I only baked them so it would give him an excuse to stop by for a cookie and chat. I asked him if I could take him and Eve out for brunch on Sunday. He said he'd check with Eve and call me.

I keep thinking, if I hadn't baked the cookies, if he hadn't stopped to chat, if I hadn't prolonged the conversation—maybe the other car wouldn't have been in his path when he lost control. Maybe everything would have turned out differently."

Margo recognized her magical thinking, her attempt to keep Carl alive if she simply hadn't brought cookies to the office. "Angela, I don't think so. None of us have the power to control things like that accident."

She ignored Margo. "Carlo's been driving that same route for years. He knows it with his eyes closed," she said, using the present tense, as if he were still alive, and calling him Carlo, his baptismal name, as though death had regressed him to her baby. "No one knows what made him veer out of lane. Maybe he was trying to avoid a squirrel or a deer. It was the injuries from the crash that killed him. No one knows what happened before the cars collided."

While she described the moments in the office when Carl was still alive, she was able to find the words and speak coherently, as if she had the power to choose an alternate ending. When she got to the moment when she had to acknowledge her son was dead, she was unable to formulate the words into sentences. There were only those primitive noises seeded in every mother's grief.

In fits and starts, Margo learned … no autopsy report yet … takes so long … Carlo was healthy … not overweight like Paul … She had taken the dog for a walk. When she got back, she kicked off her shoes and put a tv dinner into the microwave. That Friday night was like every other Friday night. Alone. By eight she was in bed with the tv on. When the doorbell rang, she looked out the window from the second-floor bedroom. A police car was parked in front of the house, its lights flashing. She put on her robe and went to the door thinking perhaps her neighbor had once again reported her cat missing. There were two policemen at the door. They had come from Eve's, where she had just learned she was a widow.

Once again, Margo kept in close contact with Angela. Each time she dialed her number and anticipated her voice, she remembered the story of the Orca printed in the *New York Times* years earlier. A thirteen-thousand-pound white whale was tracked for seventeen days, carrying her dead calf on her head.

She swam over a thousand miles through the churning waters of the Pacific Northwest, before relinquishing its dead body to the sea.

Perhaps whales are genetically predisposed to mourn for a thousand miles or seventeen days. Margo didn't know. But she did know from losing her own infant over thirty years ago, a mother who has lost a child never lets go. Angela was carrying Carlo with her, the same way she carried Paulo with her, in her head, in her heart, in the muscles of her thighs as she limped through each day.

Chapter Nineteen

2015

A week's worth of newspapers, wrapped in their plastic sleeves, lay in a pile alongside the front door when Margo rang the bell. Angela, still in her bathrobe, her hair disheveled, her eyes red from crying, finally answered. They embraced. There was no need to ask her how she was doing. Her bad days were written all over her. Margo followed her into the kitchen where the table was strewn with piles of sympathy cards, memorial gift cards, charitable donation cards in Carl's memory and Mass cards. On the floor nearby, there were two cardboard boxes with the preprinted response cards Margo had come to help her organize and address. It had been so many years since she's been in that kitchen. The past flooded her as her eyes found the oak sideboard they had discovered together, in an antique store, long before everything went bad. It still held a prominent place in her kitchen, laden with photos of the family. Margo's breath caught in her throat when she saw the wooden plaque, still centered on the wall above the sideboard, *Friendship—A Reason, A Season, A Lifetime.*

Angela lifted the kettle from the back of the stove and asked, "Cup of tea?"

Margo thought of all the cups of tea they shared; at the School for Brides, in their little Brooklyn apartments, in back-yards, at Bella Napoli, and then at Lunello. Never could she have imagined this scene, Angela's trembling hands as she tipped the boiling water into two mugs. The task ahead of them. They sat facing each other, neither of them knowing how to begin, when Angela mumbled "Last week Eve asked me to help her select a headstone. It was a real surprise, to be invited, after the fiasco of the funeral."

"Fiasco of the funeral? What are you talking about? The funeral Mass and everything else was beautiful."

She shook her head as if in disbelief. "You just don't know what I went through with Eve."

"What happened?

"I assumed Carl would be buried alongside Lou and Paul in the family plot. But no, Eve insisted on a different cemetery. Didn't you notice?"

Margo had noticed. She'd mentioned it to Kevin when they found themselves standing in the bitter cold cemetery the day Carl's casket was lowered into the ground. It was not where they stood fourteen months earlier for Lou's interment. She should have realized how upsetting that would have been to Angela. She remembered Lou joking one night at Lunello's, years earlier, about his newest real estate venture. "It's prime property and cost a fortune," he bragged. Margo and Kevin both thought he had invested in a beach house or a mountain cabin when he made his announcement; but no, he had purchased a family burial plot. "There's room for all of us," he said gleefully, as Angela shook her head at his macabre humor. He'd put the deed in a safe deposit box for some unimaginable future. Sooner than anyone could have predicted, the deed was retrieved, first for Paul, and then two years later when Lou was buried.

"It didn't make sense to me to separate Carl from his father and brother, "Angela continued, "but Artie and Rob urged me to just go along with Eve. I did."

"But it was different when you went to select a headstone with her?"

"Yes, at first." Eve had made an appointment in advance. Angela picked her up and they drove to the stonemasons together. They sat side-by-side as the salesman showed them his samples of granite, stone, and marble. It was hard, but they were united in wanting the best, the finest stone available for Carl's grave, whatever the cost.

"Our knees were touching under the little table in the office as we looked at the brochures and samples of stone. Eve didn't pull away and neither did I. At one point, she reached for my hand and held on to it. It was the first time I really felt close to her."

"I can understand how huge that little gesture was, Angela."

"We agreed on a beautiful black marble headstone, and together we carefully composed the inscription to be carved onto it.

Born April 4, 1965 – Died October 14, 2014
Carlo Romano
Loving Husband of Eve
Beloved Son of Angela and Lou Romano
Loving brother of Paul, Artie, & Rob,
Forever In All Our Hearts.

"But as always with Eve, the warm moment didn't last long."

"What do you mean?"

187

"As we got up to leave, the salesman said 'I can have it ready for you in April.'"

Eve slumped in her chair, "April. That's six months from now. Why will it take so long?" she demanded.

"He explained how they first had to acquire the marble which would take a few months. In addition, there were a lot of jobs before ours, and even if he could expedite it, the cemetery would not let them install it until the ground thawed. That wouldn't be till spring.

It was then Eve angrily announced she was selling the house and moving to California before the end of the year. She stood up, grabbed her purse, and said defiantly, "I want it installed before I leave."

Startled by this news, Angela blurted, "You're moving to California"?

Angela felt dizzy with the surprise at the announcement. She used the few minutes, during which Eve argued with the salesman for an earlier installation date, to calm herself. When they got into the car, Angela brought it up, "It's so soon to make that decision Eve. Don't you think you should give yourself some time?"

There was no talking Eve out of her decision. She was going back to California where she could be close to her mother and sisters. 'There's no reason for me to stay in New Jersey. There is nothing here for me.' She'd already had the house appraised. It was going on the market the following week.

"I wanted to shout at her" Angela said. "PARC Labs is here. Carl's brothers are here, I'm here. But I didn't. Instead, with every effort I could muster, I took Eve's hand and told her there would always be a place for her in the family, in the business. I told her to remember that."

Margo looked at Angela, over the mugs of tea neither of them had touched, over the piles of cards strewn on the table.

"Perhaps we should save these for another day," she said to Angela, as she absorbed her struggle.

"No," Angela said. "You came all the way down here to help me. Let me go wash my face and get out of this bathrobe, and then I'll be ready."

As the real estate agent predicted, the house sold quickly. Eve's mother stayed on after the funeral. They both wanted to be back in California before Christmas. Eve let it be known she wanted the estate settled before they left. She wanted to know where she stood financially. She didn't want the pressure of returning to New Jersey to sign papers after the holidays.

"We understood," Angela said. "As much as it hurt, we did everything we could to get the estate settled quickly for her." Eve had no idea what Carl's shares in the business were worth; she had no idea she needed her own attorney to represent her. PARC LAB's attorney, Michael Imbrogio, went out of his way to find someone to represent her. Thinking Eve would be most comfortable with a woman, Michael recommended Janet McTigue, a woman partner in a firm specializing in estates.

"That was really nice," Margo murmured.

"Eve liked Janet. They had a good rapport or as good as Eve was capable of during that time."

Understanding Eve's desire to leave for California before Christmas, the two attorneys worked day and night to accommodate her wishes. There were complicated buyout stock agreements that had to be set up, since Carl shared ownership in the company with other family members. An audit had to be performed to determine the value of the company before the buyout number could be determined.

Just four weeks later, Tom Olsen, PARC Labs accountant/co-director, and the two attorneys, Michael and Janet, met with Eve and her mother at the house. A preliminary copy of the buyout agreement was ready for Eve. Before handing her the contract, Janet told Eve that according to the company audit, Carl's stock was valued at ten million dollars. However, in view of the tragic circumstance surrounding Carl's accident, the PARC Lab's Corporation was prepared to give her twenty million dollars. Michael told her the contract he was leaving with her reflected the twenty million. "Look it over, and don't hesitate to call Janet or me if you have any questions or concerns." The following week, Eve called Janet and indicated she was satisfied with the buyout agreement. She was ready to move forward and settle the estate.

Family members who held shares in the company needed to be present to co-sign at the final settlement. That included Angela. The attorneys coordinated a meeting with everyone for the following Friday at Eve's house, two full weeks before Christmas.

Steeling herself to visit the house for the first time since Carl's death and the last time before it would be emptied out, Angela dreaded the meeting. That afternoon, Rob picked her up at four. As they pulled up in front of the dark house, she thought of previous Christmases, when Carl strung thousands of lights along the rooftop and decorated the lawn with a life-size nativity scene. It was as if all the life and light had been sucked out of the house.

Eve's mother opened the door and ushered them towards the dining room table, where Eve and the two attorneys were waiting. As they walked through the house, Angela glanced into the library and could see Carl's drafting table, filled with half-finished plans for a greenhouse he was designing for their back-yard. Everything about his life was unfinished. It broke her heart all over again.

The brocade curtains in the dining room were pulled shut. The rug had been rolled up and tied with cord for removal.

The meeting didn't take long. They all signed the estate papers where the lawyers told them to. It was over in less than an hour. The estate was settled. Only two months had passed since Carl's death.

Earlier in the day, Rob had made a dinner reservation for the whole group for when the meeting ended. "We asked Eve and her mother to join us, but Eve wasn't up to it, which I understood," Angela said. "I didn't want to go myself. Just the thought of food made me nauseous."

Within a week, the contents of the house were packed in a moving truck and Eve and her mother boarded a plane for California. The morning they left; Angela drove to the house to say good-bye. Eve promised to return in the spring when the headstone was installed. "I held her close," Angela said, "and again told her, you will always be a part of this family."

"THE UNMARKED GRAVE TORTURES ME. I AM COUNTING THE weeks until the headstone is installed," Angela told Margo in the weeks that followed. Margo understood. Life can be made endurable by a short-term goal, something to look forward to; a wedding, a birth, a graduation from college, the CT-scan that shows the cancer gone, a return from the Army. There are even those who seem able to forestall their own death as they wait for a loved one to arrive for the last good-bye. For Angela, looking forward to the day the headstone would be installed, and Carl's name and his life on this earth acknowledged in the marble, helped her get through the winter and early spring.

Each week she visited the cemetery with flowers, with wreaths, with prayers. Each week, as spring approached, she anticipated the call that the headstone was ready to be installed. Her frequent visits resulted in her being befriended by the caretakers at the cemetery. Aware of her frustration, they tried to help. One afternoon while she was pulling up some onion grass poking out of the dirt, they came and gently fit a rectangle of sod on top of the soil. "It looked better," Angela said, "but there's no way of knowing that it's my Carlo in that unmarked grave. I'm his mother, he lived inside me for nine months, still I have no rights regarding his death. Sometimes I want to scream to the world, this spot marks the tragedy of my youngest son, but it's Eve, his widow, who has usurped my rights."

"I don't understand," Margo said, "usurped your rights. I thought the installation was dependent on the delivery of the stone."

"The stone is in, packed in a crate at the stone mason's facility. I called them a couple of days ago and was told the order to install it was put on hold, indefinitely."

"Why? Who put it on hold?"

"I asked the same question," a furious Angela told Margo. "I was informed, 'The widow, the other Mrs. Romano told us not to do anything until she called again.'" Angela offered to sign for it, pay for it, but was told it couldn't be released and installed without Eve's signature.

"Why would she do that?" Margo asked.

"Why does she do half the things she does? She couldn't get away from us fast enough."

"What do you mean? What things?"

"She's just being spiteful." Angela said in an anger that quickly mutated to tears. "And we have been so good to her. She is a rich woman because of us."

"Yes, I remember you telling me about how generous PARC Labs was when the estate was settled."

"She not only inherited the house but over twenty million dollars. We gave her much more than we had to. Now, on some weird whim, this cancellation of the headstone."

It seemed to Margo there had to be more to this than Angela was revealing. Why was Eve being so difficult? When she asked Angela why Eve would be so uncaring, the answer was "because she's a spiteful bitch." That was as far as Angela would go.

OVER THE NEXT SEVERAL MONTHS, EACH TIME THEY TALKED, some oblique reference to the gravesite came up. It made no sense to Margo, from all that she had gleaned about the couple, that Eve would leave her husband's gravesite unfinished. Just as she had wondered about the secrets surrounding the Christmas Eve meeting in1998, that altered her son's life, she fantasized about Eve's reasons.

She had witnessed first-hand Eve's shock and distress at Carl's wake. She'd noted the wall of protection Eve's mother and two sisters built around her with their bodies. Eve's obvious devotion to Carl had been validated for her when she read the array of beautiful testaments to Carl and Eve, as a couple, posted on the funeral home website in the days following the accident. She fantasized Eve was still so fragile in her grief that she was not strong enough, mentally, or physically to travel from California. But she could imagine no fantasy to accommodate Angela's anger and her "spiteful bitch" comment.

As 2016 morphed into 2017, Angela spoke less frequently about Eve and about the headstone. Vague references to "the killing she made when she sold the house," and "the gold-digger out to ruin our family" were tossed like little bombs into their conversations and then abandoned. They came so seamlessly and so out of context that Margo sometimes wondered if she really heard them at all. Whatever was going on with Eve was just one bead in the necklace of depression choking Angela's every moment. Her life was literally frozen in place. As time went on, allusion to Eve surfaced like pesky bugs Angela swatted away with a few well-chosen words.

Margo could support Angela without knowing details. She could listen. Angela had, more than once, said "besides Father

Rich, you are the only person I talk to." When it came to Eve, she wasn't really talking. She alluded to things more sinister but was unable or unwilling to go further. Like a tv screen, flickering into pixels, the picture was always distorted as Margo tried to find a word, any word, to fill the emptiness of Angela's unrelenting sadness.

Chapter Twenty

2016-2018

M argo was up to her ankles in water after an errant sock gummed up the works of the washing machine and caused it to overflow. When the phone rang, she answered with an abrupt "hello."

"Can you talk now," Angela asked, their usual way of beginning a chat.

"I'm in a mess here. Can I call you back?"

"Yes, I have something I can't wait to tell you."

It was probably an hour later, with the mop up completed, and the plumber on his way, that Margo dialed Angela's number. She could tell from the lilt in her voice when she picked up the phone, she was excited. "The headstone was installed on Carl's grave this week. It's finally done. After four years of my fighting for it, I finally have some closure."

"It's been so long since you brought it up, Angela, I'd forgotten it was still a problem."

"Oh yes. That woman finally got what she wanted; she took us to the bank. Now that she has bled us dry and has all she wants, she allowed the headstone to be released and installed."

Margo had stopped asking her about Eve. Aside from a few sarcastic asides that occasionally slipped into the conversation, Angela rarely mentioned her. Margo had assumed somewhere in the past four years, the situation of the headstone was resolved, and Eve was out of her life.

Perhaps the easy way Angela said, "she took us to the bank," gave Margo a freedom she hadn't felt before when it came to directly asking a personal question. "Did she actually sue you?"

"Oh yes. She's been torturing us with a lawsuit, slandering me and the family and the business. Now it's over. She's finally out of our lives."

"Why would she do that?"

"Because she's a gold-digging bitch, that's why."

"Those are strong words coming from you."

"Not strong enough, as far as I'm concerned. All the money from the sale of Carl's house, twenty million dollars from the business, and still she wanted more. You never really know what someone is capable of. We had to sell a big chunk of the business to give her what she demanded."

"You sold a big chunk of PARC Labs? When?" Hearing this was more shocking to Margo than Angela's persistent vehemence towards Eve.

"Yes, we sold the pharmaceutical line to pay her off. It was just not something I wanted to talk about. It would have killed Lou if he weren't already dead. Eve got what she wanted. As a result, I finally have my son's name carved above his grave—but she did extract some final revenge."

"What do you mean?'

"Do you remember the inscription for the headstone Eve and I wrote together the month after Carl died?

"Yes," Margo said, remembering the moment that had so affected Angela, when her knees and Eve's knees were touching in the stonemason's office and Eve reached for her hand.

"She changed it. Cut out any reference to the family. Now under the dates, the inscription reads:

April 4, 1965 - October 14, 2014
Carl Romano
Loving Husband and Best Friend.

"That's it. No mention of Lou or me or his brothers. It's as though we never existed, that he was dropped into this world and had no one until she came along when he was forty years old. But I can't do anything about that. I'm just happy we are done with her. I doubt I'll ever see or hear from her again."

"Did you see her at the cemetery when the headstone was installed?'

"No, she didn't bother to show up. It was just Artie, Rob, and me."

Margo wanted to ask about the lawsuit. How had it come to this? Angela's words, "She got what she wanted," kept playing in her mind, like the refrain of some country western song. They implied the lawsuit was settled in Eve's favor, to the extent that PARC Labs sold their core pharmaceutical business to settle with her. All the years of listening hadn't prepared Margo for this.

"Did PARC go out of business?" she asked with growing horror. "Did you have to fold up the company?"

"No, no, nothing like that. We're still doing fine. PARC Labs is still standing."

Margo had so many questions. But in the moment Angela called to share happy news, Margo didn't want to take a chance of bringing her friend to a dark place by asking her to revisit the last few years. She was curious and hoped Angela would say more. During the years of their estrangement, and even when their friendship resumed, other than the lingering question that surfaced from time to time about the Christmas Eve meeting, she had no reason or desire to gather more information about the business. They rarely talked about it, other than in very general terms, so she wouldn't have known if the business had expanded over the years into new areas that were now sustaining it.

All Margo knew for sure, from what Finn had witnessed, was that when Lou made the decision to sell Bakers Palette, the company dropped their expansion plans with the confectionary brand and retreated to the original core pharmaceutical business. Now, learning of the sale of the pharmaceuticals, she wondered what was left. Something didn't compute. It bothered her, like an itch she couldn't resist scratching. But once again, some inner monitor kept her from probing.

In the silence that followed, Angela surprised her by what she did say. "You know Margo, I've come to realize, a family business isn't good for the family."

This was one of the most personal and telling statements Angela had ever made. It shocked Margo. She was such a private person; it often seemed as if Angela was speaking in code. This was so direct.

"I always thought the family business was what you and Lou dreamed of from the earliest days."

"In the beginning, it was. As the years went by, I don't know. It's hard working with your sons, day in, day out. Lou wasn't easy to please. He did things his way."

This revelation from Angela seemed to be a leap into new territory. It was as though some inner lock had been released allowing Angela to speak freely. "He didn't take advice and discounted much of what the boys had to say. He'd get angry at them for one thing or another and it caused problems for all of us."

Margo learned there were no boundaries between work and family. No time to just be a family, without the business being the God who ruled the kingdom. The boys were unhappy. They carried their frustrations into their homes. It interfered with their marriages. It kept all her daughters-in-law on the outside. They never felt part of things and didn't understand the business always came first. "They liked what PARC Labs gave them in terms of material things," Angela said. "The big house, the cars, the horses, vacations. But in the end, it caused them to resent me and Lou."

"I had no idea, Angela. I always envied you, having them all so close."

"We thought a family business was the glue that would keep us all connected and the boys financially secure. If I had it to do all over again ..." she sighed.

From the outside it had all appeared so different. Angela and Lou had strived for a family business since the boys were in diapers. They had done all the right things to achieve their goals. Now, here was her friend, who wanted nothing more than a big extended Italian family she could gather round her, stranded at the altar of regret. Her life was so diminished by loss: her husband dead, one son who left the business to save himself, two sons dead, two daughters-in-law gone their own way, and grandchildren torn from her life through divorce. Now another stunning loss, as the business gasped from the impact of Eve's lawsuit that took them down like the iceberg that crashed into the Titanic.

MARGO'S CURIOSITY ABOUT WHAT WAS SUSTAINING THE business, after this recent sale to settle with Eve, trumped her reluctance to tread any further. It was twenty-years ago when Lou announced he'd been following Finn's career on the Internet. At the time, she secretly judged him for trolling and invading her son's privacy. Bending her own self-imposed privacy rule, she sat down at the computer that evening and typed in PARC Labs. Pages of references lit up the screen. Before she could scroll to the official site, her eyes were drawn, with the force of magnets, to bold type, half-way down the page:

Widow Says Husband's Family Co. Shorted Her on Hubby's Stock Value

Blood rushed to her head. The part of her that felt she had no right to know any more than Angela chose to reveal wrestled with the voyeuristic part of her. The voyeur won. She clicked on the site and started to read, cheeks burning like a teen-ager with a page of pornography.

Initially, she thought the information was unrelated. Some other PARC Labs? The article referred to the plaintiff as Langly. It took her a few minutes to realize Eve had used her maiden name in the lawsuit. As she read, Margo recognized much of the content. It matched what Angela told her a few years earlier, during the weeks when Carl's estate was being settled. It included PARC Labs recommending Janet McTigue to represent Eve. It listed two pertinent meetings with Eve. The first, on November 11, a mere month after the fatal accident, when PARC attorney Michael Imbrogio, the accountant/co-director Tom Olsen, and Janet McTigue, the attorney representing Eve, were present. It confirmed that it was during this meeting, the buyout offer for Carl's stock was presented, offering Eve twenty million dollars. It chronicled a second meeting at the end of November, again at Eve's home, when the family was also present, in addition to the two attorneys, and the accountant. It was during this meeting, the buyback papers were signed, and the estate settled.

But there was more. Like a painting after the final brush-strokes are applied, a new picture began to emerge as Margo continued to read. In the legal suit filed with the court, Eve claimed that under a shareholder's agreement she subsequently reviewed several months later, the settling of Carl's estate was done improperly. During that first meeting, when the buyout proposal was presented, Eve claimed she asked the two attorneys, Michael and Janet, if she had any responsibilities regarding the estate. They both told her not to worry, that "Everything will be alright." When, according to her affidavit, she asked specifically how her husband's shares would be valued, she was informed that a shareholder's agreement "predetermined the terms of any sale." In essence the value of the shares was "non-negotiable." Eve claimed that she was assured the buyout agreement of twenty million represented a generous offer since Carl's stock was valued at ten million dollars, half the amount she was being offered. The fact that her own attorney, Janet McTigue, had reviewed the proposal prior to the meeting, was reassuring to Eve at the time. One last brushstroke to this new canvas of information included Eve's recollection that she felt rushed signing the final papers because "the family was late for a dinner reservation."

In her complaint, Eve stated a later review by PARC Labs own appraiser gave a fair market value to the stock she had handed over for twenty million, as valued at thirty million dollars. The language that followed in the complaint was formal, legalistic, and stunning. It included "breach of fiduciary duty," "violations of the Security and Exchange Act," "acting out of avarice, expediency, and self-interest," and "undervalued stock." It was the last accusation, "undervalued stock," that caught Margo's attention. It so resonated with echoes of Artie's complaint when he broke with his father.

The lawsuit was filed in October of 2016, just three days shy of the two-year anniversary of Carl's death. Margo wondered about the timing of Eve's lawsuit, if two years was when the statute of limitations to file a suit ran out? Aghast by what she was reading, she realized the trauma this must have caused Angela. Yet, she had never directly talked about. Margo had no doubt that Angela believed Eve was treated with compassion and generosity. Margo knew firsthand, following Carl's death, Angela was barely interested in living, much less concerned with undervalued stock. She also knew Angela was invested in maintaining her relationship with Eve, the living link to her dead son. What could have gone so wrong?

Margo asked herself, "Do I really want to know this?" The lawsuit was now history. She already knew from Angela that the case was settled. Eve had "taken them to the bank." Her relationship with her daughter-in-law had gone down like a stone in a river. The business would survive. The headstone was in place. Angela sounded relieved of a burden. She sounded happy.

Margo shutdown the article quickly, furtively, but not before she printed it. She knew she would discuss it with Kevin. She needed the hard copy to refer to, to assure herself and him of what she had unearthed. Whatever business was sustaining the company would function whether she knew about it or not. She was done with snooping. That evening at dinner she told Kevin about her extraordinary conversation with Angela.

After reading the article, Kevin just shook his head in disbelief. "It never stops for her, does it? It must have been agony going through that over these past years. It's interesting to me that she waited till it was all over to tell you about it."

"Isn't that how we've always been with each other? Going way back. We never told them about your drinking until you were in recovery. They never told us they were moving until after Lou found his new job and they bought a house, or about Artie's eloping until Lou had settled the whole affair. There are so many things we never discussed, just glossed over, like when they didn't show for my graduation party or when we let them down by not taking the godparent role as seriously as they did."

"You're right." Kevin said. "Even now, we're still careful to not acknowledge our awareness of Artie's blowup with Lou when he left the business and their estrangement in the year leading up to Lou's death."

"Maybe that's what kept the friendship going. A respect for privacy, a trust that we don't have to know everything about each other."

"Well, it worked until it didn't work," Kevin said sadly.

A few days later, as Margo balled up the article, "Widow Says Husband's Family Shorted Her" to discard, the question about the sustaining business at PARC Labs erupted again, like a case of hives. The temptation to google PARC Labs' official site and satiate her curiosity cracked her resolve to leave the question unanswered. She opened the computer and typed in PARC Labs. Once again, she had access to over thirty pages of articles about the company and once again, her attention was diverted as she scrolled to the top of the first page to access the official site:

Sholeron Inc. Acquires PARC Labs Pharmaceutical Sucrose Spheres Business

She read on, digesting details of the sale of the core business in January 2016, fourteen months after Carl's death. "Tom Olsen, Vice President and Chief Financial Officer of PARC Labs announced that they made the decision to leave the pharmaceutical and nutraceutical spheres arena in order to concentrate on their fast-growing food and confectionary business."

Comments following the quote indicated Park Labs would not disclose what Sholeron paid. Margo noted Tom Olsen, who in the lawsuit filed by Eve had been identified as accountant and co-director, was now being identified as Vice President and Chief Financial Officer.

The information confirmed what Angela had told Margo.

But something was off. It indicated the company sold the pharmaceutical business completely, not just a chunk of it to pay off Eve, as Margo understood from Angela. Additionally, according to the article Margo read the previous day, Eve didn't file her lawsuit until October of 2016, nine months after the sale, and a full two years after Carl's death and the settlement of his estate for twenty million dollars. The fact that the sale was underway in the months after Carl's estate was settled, led Margo to infer the evaluation and sale of the core business was what triggered Eve's revisiting her inheritance. It implied the true worth of the company, when it was sold to Sholeron, had not been sufficiently reflected in Carl's estate and the inheritance she accepted.

If this were true, Margo had no doubt Angela was as much a victim as Eve. She had always deferred to Lou when it came to business decisions. He had built an enormously successful company. It wasn't a stretch to assume she deferred to the legal and financial professionals and their advice at the time Carl's estate was settled. During those weeks, and the months that followed, she had been consumed with grief. Margo doubted Angela was even asked for input.

Yet reading this announcement spawned a new question. Tom Olsen, in his capacity as CFO, wrote that the sale of the pharmaceuticals division to Sholeron would allow PARC Labs "to concentrate on our fast-growing food and confectionary business."

What confectionary business? Margo thought. *Hadn't they gotten out of that business in 1999, when Bakers Palette was sold?* Was that misinformation? Was it possible Lou had changed his mind and held on to Bakers Palette? Was Finn wrong?

Margo knew that after Carl's death and Artie's departure, it was Rob alone at the helm, a position, from what Angela had told her, he never aspired to. Perhaps overseeing the two lines was more than he could handle. Selling to Sholeron was a way to streamline the operation.

She had started down this slippery slope and couldn't stop herself. She opened articles, one after another. She was reading fast. It was like being on an anthropological dig, as one by one she excavated the bones of the company and with them, a history that reached back to Christmas Eve of 1998.

Chapter Twenty-One

2018

Margo scrolled to the first entry for PARC Labs. The official site. Here she discovered a trail leading her back to where it all began.

A graphic lit up on the screen. A selection of cupcakes resplendent in a rainbow of frostings rotated across the screen, a veritable cornucopia of confectionary toppings that included sprinkles, nonpareils, confectionary stars and crescent moons, crystal prisms, pearlescent beads, and candy-sanding sugars. She was momentarily baffled. Sugar products were the last thing she expected. A sense of déjà vu washed over her. Her memory unspooled a seemingly identical graphic, the one Lou displayed on the table at Lunello, when it was hot off the press twenty years ago. Yet something was different. Within a few seconds she had it. The Bakers Palette name and logo were missing. Instead, in bold print, "PARC Labs." As she continued to read, she learned PARC Labs was indeed still thriving. It was a player in the food market, not just limping along.

Her curiosity intensified. She had long believed Bakers Palette, the original confectionary line, was sold in 1999 for the windfall that ended Finn's career at PARC. Now she wondered, was her anger misplaced? Did Artie and Rob convince their father to hold on to Bakers Palette? Was Finn wrong? Was she about to face a truth that would upend what she had stubbornly clung to? She read every word searching for a link to Bakers Palette. Nothing.

She exited the site and googled Bakers Palette, expecting to find a link to PARC Labs. But no, she found a chain of bakeries and restaurants that advertised homemade and home-baked products, oven-to-door. There was no link to confectionary products that were at one time or even now, associated with PARC.

Her dig for information came to a dead end. She was over her head in piecing together the fragments from the digital depths of Google. She called Finn and left a message to get his take on the electronic unravelling that was so immersing her. When he called back, she told him about her scavenging for information and asked, "Did you know PARC Labs is no longer in pharmaceuticals but is strictly a confectionary company?"

"Can't be," he said, when she told him the confectionary business was now the core business. "I know Lou got out of that business when he sold Bakers Palette in 1999."

"Google PARC Labs for yourself. Maybe I'm missing something, but it looks to me like the company is now totally focused on confectionary products."

"I haven't thought about this in twenty years, Mom. I know the brand was sold to an international food company based in London and they folded it into their product line to eliminate the competition. Over the years, the parent company was sold, I believe to an Indian spice company. After that, I lost track of them."

"I'm googling it now … you're right. This is interesting. I had no idea." Finn paused as he continued to read through the web site.

"What do you make of this? Do you think the sale didn't go through?"

"No, the sale went through. There is no question in my mind about that. All I can imagine is that Lou signed a non-compete with the people who bought Bakers Palette. When the non-compete ended, he would have been free to go back into that business. That's probably what he did. Nothing wrong with that. It's perfectly legal."

"Ah, it's starting to make sense." Margo knew a little bit about non-compete agreements from Kevin's business. They came up in the context of buy-sell insurance for the surviving partners of a business. He was often consulted for his accounting expertise when contracts were being negotiated. She knew they were time bound and the amount of time decided on was discretionary. Five years, ten years, fifty years? The number was arbitrary and subject to negotiation. But once the time limit expired, it was an open market once again for the seller.

Margo continued to scroll. Tucked away on one of the last of the thirty pages of entries, she excavated two more bones buried at the site of her archeological dig. The first announced:

PARC LABS Trademark Applications for Bakers Palette

As she read, more pieces started to fall into place. "There was a trademark application filed by PARC Labs for Bakers Palette in April of 2010." She continued to read aloud to Finn from the record of the application, "intended to cover the category of edible decorations for bakery goods and ice cream."

"That's interesting," Finn said. "Was there any mention of the original trademark?"

"Yes. It indicates that it was granted in 1997."

"That's when we first launched Bakers Palette. What's the status now?"

"The current status of both is listed as dead/cancelled."

"Well, the new trademark application was filed in 2010, ten years after I left. A reasonable time for a non-compete to expire and leave Lou free to go back into the confectionary business."

"I wonder why they didn't get the trademark again, why it was cancelled?"

"Wasn't it in November of 2010 when Paul died?" Finn asked.

"Yes. Do you think Lou withdrew the second trademark application when Paul died?"

"I don't know, but I imagine his death threw the company into turmoil."

It wasn't hard for Margo to understand how losing their son might have brought all PARC Labs projects to a halt that year. Another link Margo had unearthed earlier was Paul's obituary, listed several pages into the references. She read it to Finn:

Passing of Paul Romano, Vice President PARC LABS

"I didn't know Paul joined the company all those years ago," Finn said.

"Neither did I. It never came up in our conversations after Lou's death. I was shocked when I read it in the obituary."

"What I do know is that it would have made Angela and Lou very happy having all four boys working with them," Finn added.

"Yes, that would have been nirvana for them. This is how I see it, Finn, the business plan you developed, and the sale of Bakers Palette earned Lou a windfall, allowing him to begin his philanthropic endeavors. It also gave him an option for the future, going forward with the confectionary products under the PARC labs name when the non-compete expired."

"I doubt that was his plan, Mom. It probably evolved over time as the non-compete ran out."

"You're probably right," Margo said, as she told Finn about another link, buried even deeper in the google search results:

PARC LABS Completes Expansion

The article reported that in 2005, a good five years after the sale of Bakers Palette, the one-million square-foot multibuilding expansion to the facility was completed, vastly increasing both production and warehouse space to one-and-a-quarter million square-foot existing plant.

"Interesting," Finn said. "If the non-compete ran out five years after the sale of Bakers Palette, Lou may have started to expand and revisit what we had started. Nothing wrong with that. Good for him. And it looks like he did some good stuff with his profits."

"Yes, the philanthropy continued. Lou's obituary listed too many for me to remember."

"It makes me happy to know that" Finn said. "As for me, I'm long over it. I was warned about getting involved in a family business. I should have paid attention to my own gut. It seems to have worked out for him, and it worked out for me. The break in your friendship was the only real fallout, and for that I am still sorry."

"In terms of the success of the business, yes, it worked out. But their lives, so much loss. And they never got to retire. Angela's statement about a family business not being good for the family continues to haunt me."

"Why are you so interested in this, mom? Why is it so important to you? I barely remember it."

"I feel like I'm filling in the blanks of a puzzle I abandoned, solving a mystery and getting closer to understanding the friendship."

Margo could sense Finn's shrug of acceptance over the phone. It was so much less important to him, even though three years of his life had been interrupted. How could she explain it to him, to herself? It was a curiosity that despite knowing how a story ends, sent her back to the newspaper each morning to understand the details of what motivates behavior and underlies an event. A curiosity that kept her attentive to the slightest thread of a client's story, like a throwaway phrase, that might help resolve an issue. In her relationship with Angela and Lou, the story remained unfinished. It was as though she had entered a new dwelling place with her friend, intent on reestablishing their earlier bond. Yet, at times, Carl's verbal attack and Lou's indifference that Christmas Eve, wafted in the air like the scent of mold on a basement wall.

"At this point, it's just a question hanging out there. A loose end, like Charlie's golf clubs." Finn knew what she meant, and they both laughed. She and Kevin had another long-term couples' friendship, Gail and Charlie. They had been a part of their lives for as many years as Lou and Angela. The family lore around Gail and Charlie was related to a set of golf clubs Gail's parents gave to Charlie in the late sixties, to make amends for some awful thing they had done to him. All those years ago, Margo asked Gail, "Whatever did they do?"

"I can't."

Margo understood. To reveal the experience would be betraying her parents. Gail promised. "Someday I'll tell you." Now she doesn't even remember what the awful deed was. But Margo still remembers the open question. The answer to it means absolutely nothing. It has become a joke between them. Gail and Margo tease each other, and the past floods back on memory's bright waves. There are open questions and then there are closed questions, still begging to be answered.

"I would just like to find an answer to the open question that takes up space in my head," she said to Finn.

Chapter Twenty-Two

2018

With the gravestone finally in place, and the lawsuit settled, a lightness began to seep into Angela and Margo's conversations. Margo heard Bruce Springsteen or Frank Sinatra singing in the background on their calls, as Angela traded music for the silence that had been her companion. She joined a Weight Watchers' group and lost thirty pounds, started going for walks with a friend, and took knitting lessons. No longer perceiving the other couples at St. Augustine's as ignoring her because she was a widow, she dug deep into her isolation and said "Yes," to an invitation to join the group for dinner after a Saturday evening Mass. Perhaps the most telling was the birthday party she planned for herself. She hired limousines to ferry the far-flung grandchildren. It was the first time she had allowed herself to celebrate anything since Lou and Paul's death in 2012.

"You'd be proud of me, Margo," she said, "I went to the garden center this week to buy a new glider for the deck." A small thing for a woman who could afford anything, but a huge accomplishment when looked at from the perspective of what it meant, this indication Angela was planning a future.

"I started talking to another shopper, a nice-looking man about my age. We were comparing the finish and the cushions, and for the first time in years, I thought about sharing a porch swing."

"Why, Angela, you were flirting!"

"Well, maybe I was," she laughed as she recognized the spark of interest ignited at the garden center. It was a lovely moment. Margo felt as though they had slid back into the fifties; two girls, talking about flirting with boys, before embarking on a future more complicated than any twenty-one-year-old imagines. Perhaps it was the spell of recapturing a past that had been found and lost and found again. Margo felt as close to Angela, as she had when Angela trekked with her to a doctor appointment in the mid-nineties, when Margo was worried about a lump in her breast, or those stolen moments of "telephone tea" after the kids went off to school, or the evenings they spent at the School for Brides. It was a natural moment, no more complicated than coming upon the trowel that was buried in the garden all winter, not because discovering it will change your life, but for that sense of finding what you didn't know you'd lost.

Buoyed by the old feelings of familiarity, without forethought or plan, Margo was as surprised as Angela to hear what came out of her own mouth, "Angela, there's a question I've been wanting to ask you for twenty years, but I've always been afraid to ask it."

"Really? What? Ask me anything. I'll tell you."

Unlike years ago, when she rehearsed the question, carried it on the tip of her tongue to those dinners at Lunello, now she didn't know how to put the words together. Uppermost in her mind was, why did Carl attack Finn at that Christmas Eve meeting in 1998? She immediately rejected starting with that.

Carl was dead. Angela might not know what happened in that meeting. Why would she even believe her? Margo could hear her own heart beating loudly as her mind raced to construct the question in a way devoid of judgment, more an invitation….

"It's about all those years ago when Finn went to work at PARC. He was there about two years and then everything changed. I never understood what happened."

There was silence. Margo could tell Angela was peeling back wooly layers of memory. Finally, she said, "He was unhappy, Margo. You told us that night at Lunello when we talked about recruiting him, that he had always dreamed of running a small company. But he wasn't happy, we could tell. There were five of us and one of him. It's hard being in the middle of someone else's family. It wasn't his family. He wanted to leave. It was the right thing."

Margo knew that to be true. In the months before Finn left, he was very unhappy. But she also knew for the prior eighteen months things had been wonderful, until that meeting, in a betrayal that was never understood or explained. The warmth generated by that close moment on the phone combined with the old curiosity and instinct to right her son prevailed. Angela's explanation, "he was unhappy," implied that Finn had changed since signing the contract to work at PARC. Yet Margo knew it was Lou and the business plan that had changed around him.

The old questions swirled like fraught bees escaping a hive that someone had disturbed… *Why did Carl attack Finn? Why didn't Lou stop him? Why did Lou sell Bakers Palette without informing Finn? Why was it ignored in all their conversations?*

THERE ARE TIMES IN LIFE WHEN A SUDDEN GRACE DESCENDS, and we know something we didn't know before. It is not anticipated or planned for, and it is only in retrospect that we realize we have been changed. It was only later that evening, as Margo recounted the phone conversation to Kevin that she found herself calling it grace.

Buoyed by the closeness they had rebuilt over the years and Angela's trusting "Ask me anything. I'll tell you," Margo was perilously close to leading her friend into the labyrinth of 1998. Any one of those swirling questions would lead Angela to piercing the cocoon she had spun to protect the best years of her life, when her four boys and her husband were alive, long before the sorrows that unfolded like an Italian opera were forced upon her. As she sifted through the questions some unexpected grace must have informed her that her questions were much more than questions. They were statements of her truth disguised as questions. Relics from 1998; a narrative she'd constructed and called absolute truth.

Emily Dickinson wrote,

"Tell the truth, but tell it slant–
Success in Circuit lies…
The Truth must dazzle gradually
Or every man be blind–

Margo had adhered to that in her practice, as midwife to a client's pain. It was crucial to know when a patient was ready to face what may be in plain sight to those around her. Denial is a powerful defense that compels respect. It is a rare individual who can get through life without it. In the therapeutic hour, the midwifing was about the needs of the patient, but here Margo was thinking of her own need to not only have her curiosity satisfied, but to be validated in her long-held beliefs. But why?

What else could she call it but grace as she realized the truth was as useless as air escaping from a worn tire. It held no heft or purchase for anything in her life and could only hurt

Angela. The questions, like those frantic misplaced bees, returned to the hive as Margo said, "You're right Angela. Finn was unhappy before he left ... I remember that ..."

She would leave it there; a truth they could both live with.

But Angela surprised her. She had been thinking her own thoughts about Finn's unhappiness.

"We probably needed the money ..." she said quietly. "There were lots of times Lou needed money just to keep everything going and he always made his own decisions. Even with the boys. He didn't want their advice. He had his own way of doing things and he was stubborn. It caused more problems than you can imagine. There was room for everyone"

What Angela pulled from the sarcophagus of memory was something that seemed plausible to her. Margo's instinct rejected "we probably needed the money." Finn would have had an inkling, if not full knowledge, of a financial crisis since he was partnering with Lou in running the company. Yet, she knew it wasn't a lie. Angela had groped for an explanation for Finn's unhappiness that made sense to her. Yet, her revealing that Lou "didn't want advice, even from the boys," translated to something deeper. Lou's difficulty giving up control, even with his sons.

She was convinced Angela had no knowledge of Carl's outburst and Lou's failure to intercede. If she did have some second-hand knowledge from Lou or one of the boys about what had transpired, Margo believed she didn't know its impact, what it meant in the big picture for Finn. The incident had washed over her the way water washes over pebbles in a stream. She could imagine it being of such little significance at the time, Angela would have tried to smooth things over with a batch of cookies or an extra hug, never suspecting it was the beginning of the end for Finn. She wasn't downplaying the incident. It was the narrative she believed.

Margo's fantasy of Angela feeling betrayed by Finn for

leaving the company and upset with Kevin and her for not talking him out of it, bloomed once again in her mind. Her gut told her Angela never knew there was a link between the sale of Bakers Palette and Finn's being "unhappy."

Margo was confused by Angela's little throwaway sentence, "There was room for everyone," and asked Angela what she meant.

"Paul."

"Paul? I don't understand."

"After all our years of begging and cajoling him to come work with us, when he got word that his company was downsizing and he might be let go, he was finally ready to join the family business."

"Is that why Lou needed the money?"

After another pause, she answered indirectly, "Maybe. Lou didn't tell me everything." She continued, "There was room for Finn too. There would always be a place for him at PARC. I told him that before he left."

Margo didn't doubt Angela's sincerity. She recalled Angela using the same words with Eve when she left for California. The revelation about Paul, a mere addendum to their conversation, transformed itself into the missing thread in the narrative Margo had been weaving for twenty years.

She knew from Paul's obituary, read the night of her internet frenzy, he was a Vice President at PARC Labs when he had his heart attack in 2010. At the time, she didn't know when Paul came on board and just assumed it was later, during those twelve years when there was no contact. Now she learned Paul was poised to join the company at the very time the Christmas Eve meeting took place. Of all the fantasies she'd conjured, about why Lou allowed Carl to set in motion the events that led to Finn's leaving, Paul's potential position in the company was one that had never even crossed her mind.

The opportunity to have their four sons in the business after all those years, must have been a heady experience. It completed a circle. It was the golden ring on the merry-go-round Lou and Angela had coveted. Perhaps Lou saw his oldest son as the one who could eventually run the company, succeed him. From looking at the history of PARC Labs since Finn left, it was obvious that, as Finn predicted, Lou had abandoned his desire to take the company public. He never again pursued it. As a private company, he remained in control. The business flourished with Lou at the helm. For the next ten years, until Paul's untimely death, they were living their dream. Blood triumphed.

She finally had her answer. It was about keeping the family together, where Angela and Lou believed they could protect their four boys. PARC Lab was the insurance policy they believed would guarantee everyone's lifelong happiness. A perfect storm had arisen; the profit to be made selling Bakers Palette and the potential for Paul to join PARC LABS reignited the long-held dream, conceived in innocence at the kitchen table all those years ago. Finn was simply fallout.

Yet, what wasn't conceived in innocence was the way Lou allowed or even setup Carl, at that Christmas Eve luncheon, to put into motion the change of direction for the business plan. In retrospect, Margo couldn't help feeling that Carl was as much a victim of his father as Finn.

She thought about how Kevin and she would have acted in similar circumstances, knowing in both their marriages family came first. The accumulated fear she felt about ferreting out this truth seemed so unwarranted now. She wondered how different things would have been if during one of those dinners at Lunello she had simply asked the question instead of nursing it like a splinter caught under her skin.

Chapter Twenty-Three

2018

As 2018 progressed, Angela's good months started to accumulate. They spoke less frequently as Angela became more involved in stitching together the pieces of her own unraveled life. Her Christmas card, "Dearest Margo and Kevin," arrived the first week of December. But this year, unlike those years of separation when Margo was on the lookout for the card, Margo was preoccupied. It was the first of many cards that remained unopened as she plodded through the holiday season.

On Christmas Eve Day, the phone rang. "Margo, I didn't get a card from you. Is everything alright?"

It wasn't.

"Oh, I'm so sorry. So much going on. Kevin was diagnosed with cancer in early November. We're struggling."

Now the situation was reversed, and it was Angela who listened to Margo as she told her how Kevin's routine yearly physical led to some tests, and scans, and a biopsy, and finally, the dreaded diagnosis. Margo asked her questions, looking for disparities between Lou's cancer and Kevin's, desperately hoping to find something that would predict a different outcome for Kevin. In the weeks and months that followed, Angela called frequently. They had those conversations women have with each other, comparing cancer symptoms and signs, how it is all the same, it is all different, there is reason to hope, there is no reason to hope, as your head tries to make sense of a disease that breaks your heart.

During one of their calls, Margo speculated about what had caused the cancer, as if by figuring out its origins she could magically undo the wild cells ravaging Kevin's body. Angela revisited her final days with Lou and told Margo, "Lou had so much stress with the business. I guess I can't say stress caused his cancer, but sometimes I wonder, if it weren't for the business, maybe he'd still be alive. Oh well, I'll never know." And then she repeated those same words, "but what I do know is a family business isn't good for the family."

"If I had it to do all over again," Angela mused, "I don't know Margo … the business caused so much trouble between Lou and me. I didn't always agree with him. I tried to defend things the boys did, decisions they made, but Lou just got angry. The boys were always frustrated."

Margo thought she had said as much as she was going to say, but after a pause, she cleared her throat and said, what in retrospect was probably one of the hardest revelations she ever uttered.

"They just didn't live up to their father's expectations and each of them knew it."

The enormity of this simple sentence stunned Margo. Those fifteen words burned in her mind, like hot coals, rendering her speechless. As she struggled with how to respond, Angela continued, "Nothing they did was good enough. Lou tried to deny it, cover up his disappointments, but there were so many raging outbursts when his true feelings came out. It hurt them, it hurt me."

"I had no idea, Angela. I never saw that side of him, only the witty, joking side. Never even suspected that anger. Finn never alluded to it either."

"He probably never got that way with Finn. But the slightest thing would set him off with the boys. He rarely trusted their decisions. He overruled them at every turn. It had to be his way or the highway. I should have been able to confront him. Not so long ago I told Artie and Rob that I wish I had been a better mother."

"Oh, don't say that. You are a great mother. Remember, you're the one I wanted to raise my kids when I thought I was going to die in a plane crash."

"Yes, that was another lifetime ago."

Artie and Rob had told her she was crazy to think that way, she was a good mother. Yet, when she looked back, she wished she had taken more of a stand with all the criticism they had endured.

"I could feel their unhappiness, especially Artie's. It was Artie who shouldered the brunt of Lou's wrath. He had his own ideas. Rob and Carl were more like me, inclined to keep the peace. They didn't confront him. Do you remember that show from the fifties, *Father Knows Best*?"

"Yes, an idyllic family where the father solved all the problems."

"That was a code phrase between the boys and me. We used it at least once a day in the office when we wanted to scream in frustration, one of us would grit our teeth and whisper, *father knows best*."

"Is that why Artie eventually left?"

"Yes, Artie was as hotheaded as Lou. They were at each other all the time, especially after Finn left."

"In retrospect, what kept you from confronting Lou?"

"I was afraid he'd leave. He did leave a few times. I'd lived with my own father walking out on my mother more than once.

As an only child I lived in fear of that. I saw what it did to my mother. I was afraid of the loneliness."

LATER, AS MARGO WENT ABOUT HER DAY, THE CONVERSATION played itself over and over in her mind. She thought back to that night at Lunello when their friends first approached Kevin and her about recruiting Finn. Her heart had warmed when Lou said, "I will treat him as one of my own." The words echoed in some valley of regret a few years later when Finn was so disappointed. Now, in a flash of clarity, Margo saw. Lou did indeed treat Finn as "one of his own." The weight of his promise, and all it implied, broke over her in a thunderous wave of gratitude for her son's ability to extricate himself from the family dynamic that had continued to beleaguer Lou's boys.

Years earlier, when she was so angry at Lou, Margo had facetiously called him a narcissist, the way one might sarcastically use the adjective jerk or stupid to express annoyance. Now, given this window into a marriage and family where Lou's damaging behavior had reverberated on almost every level, her superficial label of narcissism turned serious. She saw what had been hiding in plain sight; manipulativeness, entitlement, the need for admiration, control, arrogance, anger, and a lack of empathy. The whole debacle of Finn's employment was illuminated in the light of a narcissistic personality disorder in ways she'd never noticed before.

A narcissist is someone who is often charming and who will make you the most important person in their world, then leave you when they have won at their game, discard you without looking back. This was confirmed in Margo's practice, as she witnessed clients, crushed by narcissistic relationships, seeking treatment to pick up the pieces of their own diminished lives. She wondered how many times Angela and her boys had been a victim of that behavior. How many times and in how many ways had Lou left Angela? How many times did she bear the burden of remaining quiet as she witnessed her son's hurt?

Margo knew, only too well, it is rarely the narcissist who seeks treatment. They do not experience their behavior as dysfunctional because it works in maintaining their hard-won equilibrium. They have no insight into how detrimental it is to others.

Narcissism is one of the hardest personality disorders to treat and the hardest to overcome. It is thought to be the relationship with parents that contaminates a child's developing personality. The child fills in the gaps around what is missing in his or her nurturing with a false self, one that allows him to have positive self-regard, where in reality, there exists shame, inadequacy, insecurity, vulnerability, and humiliation.

The more profound cases of narcissism are thought to be related to abuse, while those on the milder end of the continuum, to an overabundance of unrealistic praise. As Margo considered her armchair diagnosis of Lou, she couldn't help but wonder what constellation of parental behaviors went into warping Lou's sense of himself. What emptiness was he filling to compensate for the paucity of his own positive self-regard?

She knew his parents were still children when his grandparents immigrated from Italy. Lou was first generation American. She also knew his parents worked hard to send him to private school where his brilliance was recognized and nurtured. Yet Lou never spoke of his parents. It was as though they were dead to him. Margo tentatively brought up the subject to Angela.

"They wanted the best for him, but they went about it in the wrong way. I suppose they didn't know any better."

"What do you mean?"

"They were old school. They demanded a lot and disciplined him in awful ways. There were times his father burned him with the stub of a cigarette to teach him a lesson. Things like losing the change from a trip to the grocery story, breaking a neighbor's window while playing baseball in the street, failing to get an A on an exam. His mother never interfered or came to his rescue. He really hated his father."

Margo thought with horror of the scars she'd noticed on Lou's back the day he went into the pool to retrieve the pebbles. She asked Angela about them.

"Yes. The burns were on his back so no one else would see them."

Margo had borne witness to trauma in her hospital work as patients peeled away the history of secret abuse at the heart of their current unhappiness. There, her training allowed her to be objective in shepherding the healing process. But this was different.

"Oh my God," was all she could say.

"It finally stopped when he got to high school," Angela said. "A Jesuit priest found him crying in the chapel one afternoon and was able to pry from him the history of the abuse. He called Lou's father and that's when it stopped. Lou never forgot it. That's why he set up the scholarship fund and always supported his old high school. The Jesuits became the father his biological father was incapable of being."

"Did Lou ever use that kind of punishment on the boys?" Margo asked, knowing how the abused often become abusers, in their misguided attempts to undo the psychological damage inflicted on themselves in the past.

Angela's "no" came as a relief.

"He was flawed, like we all are, in our own way, Angela," she found herself saying, as a grief for the lost years welled up inside of her. A grief for Lou's abuse, a grief for Angela's fear of loneliness, a grief for Lou's disappointment in his children, a grief for his four boys who lost so much, a grief for the trips they didn't take, the laughs interrupted.

"We all did the best we could. We all made mistakes," she

said, knowing the wasted years could never be recaptured. She looked at her own mistake, the way she contributed to their estrangement by the anger that burned inside her, nourished by her righteousness and her fantasies, she had refused to confront Lou. She allowed twelve years to be swallowed by time without calling Angela and Angela had allowed those same twelve years to evaporate without reaching out to Margo.

A logical conclusion for Margo to draw, from all she had just learned, was that it was Lou who influenced Angela to cease responding to or contacting her. Angela confirmed what Margo suspected, Lou held Kevin and her partially responsible for not talking Finn out of leaving PARC. He had just assumed Finn would acclimate to the sale of Bakers Palette and realign his career goals at PARC under Lou's direction. Once he left, Lou never spoke of Finn again, and as with so many things in their lives, Angela followed his lead. She didn't really understand how she came to call Margo just twelve hours after his death.

"I just found myself dialing your number. I didn't even have to look it up."

"It was kind of miraculous that you reached us so quickly," Margo said, thinking how lucky they were that the telephone number remained the same after moving to the condo. A need to search for it might have been all it took for the impulse to pass and change all that came afterwards.

With the uncomfortable truths now out in the open, a swelling compassion grew inside Margo. She had never thought about forgiving Lou. Her goal was always to put aside the past, coax it into evaporating, forget what had so distressed her at one time. She had been successful at doing that during the years when Angela and she found each other again. But today was different. She learned that on the wings of compassion, forgiveness suddenly alights in the heart and makes it whole again.

Chapter Twenty-Four

2019

The following May, spring announced itself with a plethora of forsythia and cherry blossoms that competed with the long-awaited news that Kevin's cancer was in remission. Life returned to normal for Margo. There was no way of knowing how long normal would last. But this was a good day. She took advantage of it by going for a walk in the park. When she returned, Kevin said, "Angela called. Call her back. She has some news."

"Good news?"

"Not sure. Rob is moving to Florida."

"No, you must have gotten that wrong. He would never leave the business, leave her. Rob is the only son still there."

"Well, that's what she said."

"Was she upset?

"No, she seemed fine."

"She can't be fine. With Artie running his own business in Pennsylvania, who will be there for her? Who will run PARC Labs?" Margo never imagined the business going away. It had a life of its own, surviving all the losses. It was the mountain that would never topple.

"I told her you would call her back. She's leaving for a meeting with Father Rich at four and will be home tonight."

Father Rich, she thought. Angela's upset.

THEY SPOKE LATER THAT NIGHT. KEVIN HAD INDEED GOTTEN IT right. Rob and Diana were getting married. They had purchased land in Florida and were building a home there. Rob still had to sell his house in New Jersey. It would take a while. "I still have time to get used to it," Angela said with a sigh.

"What about the business?" Margo asked. "Can Rob run it from Florida?"

"Yes. He won't be leaving permanently until the house is built, which he estimates will take about a year. Meanwhile he plans to commute to Florida on the weekends. I'll still have him around for another year."

Although the news was rocking Margo, Angela did not seem distraught. Margo knew there was in Angela a deep need to conceal. Less so lately, but it was hard to know if this was one of those times. Margo had rarely seen it coming when Angela broke down on the phone. There were times, when during an innocuous conversation, without any forewarning that she was able to anticipate, Angela would dissolve in angry tears. Always the same words, "You don't know what it's like to lose your sons and a husband, Margo." Those words were like a pressure valve erupting before releasing steam.

Often, the intensity of the raw pain shook Margo. She would try to help, by conjuring any morsel of support she could find, to comfort her in that moment. These microbursts of loss and rage were quickly followed by an apology, as if having expressed herself, she reconstituted, and her emotions were filed once again in some safe order. That evening, as Angela discussed Rob moving to Florida, she remained steady and accepting.

"I'm feeling so bad for you, Angela. With Artie in Pennsylvania and Rob in Florida, will you be okay?"

"I want my son to be happy and if this makes him happy, I'm okay with it."

Here was the last son standing at PARC Labs, the one who kept it going as all the names, Paul Romano, Artie Romano, Lou Romano, and Carl Romano, one by one, were subtracted from the letterhead.

"Did you know this was coming?"

"No. Diana and Rob were on vacation in Florida and on an impulse looked at some property. It was that quick. They weren't even planning to move."

"It will be such a big change for you."

"I'll be all right, Margo. Rob deserves the chance to have his own life. He's been living Lou's life these eight years since Lou died. Florida will be good for him. After he moves, he'll run the company from Florida." Then as an afterthought, probably to appease Margo, she said with a laugh that belied the intention, "Maybe I'll even move to Florida."

They both knew that was never going to happen. Her house and PARC Labs were the anchors that kept her moored to the best days of her life. She seemed to have accepted Rob's plan. Having the year to ease into it softened the impact.

One Tuesday morning, three months later, Margo dialed Angela's number. Her phone rang and rang. This was unusual. They expected one another's calls and generally answered on the third or fourth ring.

When Angela finally picked up, she was crying. Margo could barely understand her muffled words through the phone, "Rob had a breakdown."

Margo knew "breakdown" had different connotations for different people. She didn't know what the word meant to Angela. For people who are unable to express emotions, a good cry constitutes a breakdown. But she also knew, from her clinical practice, that the most severe end of the breakdown spectrum included a total inability to function, sometimes accompanied by psychotic symptoms. From the way Angela sounded, she feared the worst.

"What do you mean?

Through her sobs, Angela haltingly told her how the previous morning, Rob had gone into the office early, to get a jump on the week. When his assistant came in an hour later, she found him in a fetal position on the floor, shaking uncontrollably. He couldn't speak or tell her what was wrong. She called 911. Rob was taken to the emergency room. He was subsequently transported to Inwood, the psychiatric hospital where Margo had worked. "They said he was catatonic. What does that even mean? They won't let me see him. I don't know what to do."

Hearing this, Margo's worst fears were confirmed. Rob's breakdown fit the severe end of the spectrum. It was serious. If he was catatonic, he was not able to speak. She tried to collect herself.

"Can I come down?"

"No, Artie is on his way. We're going to the hospital, even though the doctor said 'no visitors.' If they still don't let me see him, I'll try to meet with one of the doctors."

"It's common to restrict visitors, even family members, until someone is stabilized, Angela," Margo offered. "The hospital will figure it out, and I know from experience, Inwood is the best psychiatric hospital in the state. I imagine they will let you see him within the next forty-eight hours."

"Could you get any information? Do you know anyone who still works there?"

"I don't. It's been years since I left. But even if I did, the code for privacy around every patient would not allow for anyone to confirm Rob's status to me, or even acknowledge he's a patient."

"I so desperately want to see him."

"I know. I'd feel the same way. But meeting with his doctor is a good idea." Once again, Margo found herself asking questions: "Did you have any idea Rob was struggling? Did you see this coming?"

"Not this. I knew he was unhappy, but I thought it was about missing Diana." Margo understood as she remembered Angela mentioning that Diana had been living in Florida full-time since the house was under construction. Yet, Angela's response produced an echo in her. "He was unhappy," were the same words she used when Margo asked about Finn leaving PARC, and about Artie leaving the business.

Angela seemed to be hyperventilating through the sobs. "When I look at all Rob's been through, I should have realized just how unhappy he was. I just didn't see it. Do you remember the accident he had at the plant a couple of years ago?"

Margo did. It was just prior to Carl's death. At the wake Rob had his foot elevated on a chair, a cast immobilizing his leg from his toes to his thigh. Diana hovered over him. A week earlier, his preoccupation with fixing a broken machine caused him to misjudge his footing. His leg got caught in the grinding machinery, severing ligaments and muscle in his foot, ankle, and calf.

"I think it started then." Angela said. "He almost lost his leg, and the recuperation took a full year. With Carl gone, he was alone running the business, which was not something he ever wanted. Of all my boys he was the one least interested in being in charge. He felt all this pressure to keep it going. So many people depending on his decisions. Even though Lou was gone, he continued to strive to make his father proud."

Angela pieced the story together, trying to understand it herself as she explained it to Margo. Two years ago, when the decision was made to sell the pharmaceutical line, they all thought things would get easier. Then out of nowhere, that lawsuit from Eve. None of them ever dreamed the court would award her a settlement. Rob blamed himself for losing the case. "But it wasn't his fault," Angela said through sobs. "We got bad legal advice when Carl's estate was probated. If Lou were alive, it would have been different. He read everything. Nothing got past him. He knew the right questions to ask. I was too numb at the time to even give it any attention and Rob didn't have the background or expertise to question the advice. You know what Rob said to me during the long months of litigation?"

"No, what?"

"He said he wished Finn had never left the company. 'None of this would have happened if he were running PARC Labs,' was how he put it. Fighting that lawsuit really devastated Rob, and I don't think he ever got over it," she said with renewed bitterness.

Margo didn't know how to respond. This was the only reference to Finn's having worked at PARC Labs that Angela had ever uttered to her. At the same time, as she listened to those words, an icy fear filled her veins. She wondered if it would have been her son having a breakdown had he remained at PARC. She shook off the thought.

"I've got to go," Angela said. "Artie is here to drive me to the hospital."

"Good luck. I'll call you tomorrow."

BY THE TIME MARGO REACHED HER THE FOLLOWING EVENING, Angela had seen Rob. Upon arriving at the hospital, she and Artie waited in the reception area. Diana, who had flown up from Florida, was with Rob and there was only one visitor allowed at a time. Angela was terrified as she sat in the large reception area. An array of plants and a circle of individually potted Ficus trees soaked up sun from the wall of windows that overlooked peaceful gardens. The acres of woodlands surrounding the hospital did nothing to calm her. Other visitors sat quietly in carefully spaced enclaves of chairs, carrying their apprehensions and hope in their squared shoulders and alert gazes. From across the room, another mother made eye-contact with Angela, in a sort of solidarity. From her seat, she saw Diana being ushered into the room by a hospital volunteer. Diana was visibly upset. Her eyes rimmed in red. She had broken her eyeglasses in the rush to leave Florida. The eye strain was obvious as she squinted at Angela and Artie. She hugged them and shook her head from side to side as though defeated. "I don't know, I don't know," she murmured softly.

The volunteer led Angela to the elevator and through the locked doors of a psychiatric unit. "It was awful," Angela told Margo. "I tried not to stare at the other patients. Some were tied in wheelchairs, others talking to themselves in empty rooms or screaming, others sedated, barely awake. I passed a room where a therapist was throwing a large ball back and forth between the patients, praising those who caught the ball, encouraging those who weren't quick enough to accomplish the little task. I thought of you. How did you ever work, day after day, in a place like that, Margo?"

Her question took Margo back to the first time she entered such wards during her training. The shock, the apprehension. But even then, it was not her son locked behind those doors. The patients were strangers to her. Margo wasn't sure if the question was rhetorical or not. She answered it anyway—in an attempt to offer hope to Angela. "I watched people recover, get better, and resume their lives. That's the reward that kept me coming back." She wasn't sure if Angela heard her response or not.

When she got to Rob's room, Angela was shocked by what she saw. Her son, strapped in a chair, barely awake, sedated, drool seeping from his mouth. Yet he tried to smile. He recognized her. It broke her heart when he mouthed, "I'm sorry."

His memory of what happened was meager. Haltingly, he managed a few words … a heart attack, my chest … exploding … my head too… I couldn't talk … couldn't think … shaking uncontrollably, happened before … passed after a few minutes … But not this time."

Later, a doctor told Angela it would likely take months of treatment. She assured her "Rob will recover." That little phrase "Rob will recover," became Angela's mantra, repeated over and over throughout the slow months of hospitalization, followed by three months' participation in an outpatient day program, from which he was gradually weaned from five to two and finally one day a week.

After his discharge from the day program, Rob continued with weekly psychotherapy. Each week brought him closer to his healthy self. Margo could hear the relief in Angela's voice when, finally Rob's was well enough to ease back into his position at the helm at PARC. The Florida plan still in place; it was all going forward.

"THERE ARE NO MORE FAMILY MEMBERS AT PARC LABS," WAS the first thing Angela said, six weeks later when Margo answered the phone for their Tuesday chat. Her first thought was that Rob had a relapse. Her second thought was Rob's one-year plan to relocate and work from Florida had accelerated to the present. Yet there was something about the agitation in Angela's voice and her choice of words that alerted Margo. No, this was different. It was more like an announcement, a headline that grabbed her attention in a different way.

"Is Rob okay?"

"Yes, he is fine. There will be no commuting or working from Florida. He quit the company entirely. It's over for him. He won't be going back. His doctor and his therapist all agree that staying at the business would put him in jeopardy of a relapse. He feels good now. He's happy and he doesn't need the money. It's the right thing. Others will run it."

Then, like a carefully placed epigraph, as if she needed to utter it again, to convince Margo, to convince herself, Angela repeated, "There are no family members at PARC anymore."

"Does the company still exist? Will you be okay financially?"

"Oh, yes. It will continue without family. I'm not concerned about money. I'm set for life. But I'll tell you something that really hurts. They asked me to leave."

Margo could tell from her voice and the way she had emphatically repeated the statement about family members, this was the final blow. It was personal and it was crushing her.

"They, who are they?"

"The same employees who have been there, Tom Olsen, Michael Imbrogio, all of them... I thought they were my friends." Her voice trailed off, then picked up again, "I feel like I've been expelled, thrown out to the curb." She paused and Margo could tell she was fighting back tears.

"Do you know what I'm going to miss the most?"

"Seeing Rob there?"

"No, not that. It's the feeling I got whenever I walked into the office. Some of the staff came to us when they were very young and over the years became like my adopted children. I cared for them, and I felt they cared for me. It was the place where I still felt like I had an identity to be proud of, as a founder of the company, as Lou's wife, and the mother of the boys who ran it. I had a desk and a phone in that office for almost forty years. All my identities converged. I belonged. It was the place where our legacy continued to make a difference. Now there is nothing."

Margo wanted to counter the emptiness this latest loss had carved into her heart, fill it with all the reasons her legacy and Lou's would continue, remind her that not having a physical presence at PARC Labs didn't erase all that she and Lou had accomplished. Someday, when Angela was ready, they would have that conversation. In those moments of confronting Rob's departure from the family business and her being asked to leave, Margo knew, as Angela's friend, all she could do was be with her, bear witness as Angela allowed her into this exquisitely private ache that was so diminishing her. Their shared history, so long written in their bones, once again opened the portal to when friendship is the lifesaver the universe throws out to keep you afloat.

Chapter Twenty-Five

2020

The day came when Margo called Angela to let her know Kevin had died. They both knew it was coming. The seasons of their lives were merging once again. Margo was entering that sacred space of absence that Angela had inhabited for so many years. Knowing of her isolation from family and reluctance to drive any but local roads, Margo told her not to feel obligated to make the trip to the wake or funeral. She meant it.

As Margo followed the casket down the center aisle of the church, behind six grandsons who served as pallbearers, she was aware of the crowded church. She took her seat in the front row with her children. Their spouses and grandchildren were seated immediately behind them.

Towards the end of the Mass, as Margo knelt in prayer, friends and family made their way to the altar for Holy Communion. One by one, they filed past her after receiving the Host. During the procession of familiar faces, her eyes were drawn to a woman who caught her attention. She was dressed all in white. Not the white of a nurse's uniform or the white of a sheet, but the elegant cream color of tea roses. She wore a tailored suit with a matching blouse. Her handbag and shoes were of a soft cream leather, and she had a delicate lace veil covering the crown of her head.

Margo didn't know who she was. It was obvious from the way her eyes latched onto Margo's that she seemed to be communicating something. She was the only one in the church who had eschewed somber garb. Her clothes made a statement. She was letting everyone know she was celebrating Kevin's life, doing what she could to transform the darkness of death. In that moment, the woman veered from the procession of communicants and approached Margo, whose hands were resting on the oak rail of the first row, against which she was kneeling. The woman gently placed her hands over Margo's. She quietly bent down to kiss her. After lightly touching Maura's hands, in a gesture of condolence, she moved on. It was over in seconds. Margo still didn't know who she was. Maura and she exchanged puzzled looks. Margo had this wild thought that there are people who simply attended funerals at random, to fulfill some need to mourn, the way someone might go to a movie or crash a party.

Later, when Mass was over, Margo waited alongside the hearse, as each mourner left a flower, as they filed past the casket. The woman in white was one of them. Again, there was eye contact. Margo still could not place her. Perhaps it was the emotion of the day or seeing so many faces from her past that flummoxed her. Suddenly, the woman in white pivoted. She began to backtrack towards Margo. It was then, as from a dream, Margo saw Lou materialize alongside her. His hand was resting gently under her elbow, guiding her. The girth of his shoulders, bulging under his navy suit, the thick black hair. In one dizzying moment, reality shifted, and Margo recognized

Arturo Romano, so like his father that Margo's breath caught in her throat.

How could she have failed to recognize her? A few years ago, when Angela told her she was going to Weight Watchers, Margo cheered her progress as she shed thirty pounds, but had not seen her since she and Angela were together in the weeks following Carl's death. In the years since, they spoke continually, sharing all their trivial and intimate moments over cups of telephone tea. Margo could probably predict what Angela was feeling in any given situation and Angela knew Margo well enough to do the same.

When she told Angela about Kevin's death, Margo knew getting to the funeral, so many miles away, would overwhelm her. "Don't worry about coming. I know you're with me."

"I am, Margo. I'll attend Mass in my parish that morning. I will be with you."

And now, here she was. As Artie released her elbow, Angela reached for Margo's hands. "You didn't recognize me did you Maar-go?"

As she heard Angela's voice, and the way she said her name, with Artie standing quietly alongside her looking so much like Lou twenty years earlier, before it all went bad, a wave of joy broke over her. Margo threw her arms around her friend. She clung to Angela the same way Angela had clung to her after Lou's death. The years came rushing back.

There was a time she would have recognized Angela from the far side of a football field or the other end of a subway car, her handsome frame, her blonde hair, sensible black jacket, the small diamond she wore on her ring finger.

How much do we really know each other? Margo thought. We orbit around each other, sometimes touching, often missing, in this lifetime of reasons and seasons. Nothing had registered in the church. The weight loss disguised the sturdy frame, her hair no longer blonde was streaked with gray underneath the white veil, and the white outfit was unlike any she had seen Angela wearing except on her wedding day.

Like a stereogram, one of those pictures hidden within a picture, once you see it, you can't unsee see it.

"Stay for the repast," Margo urged.

"We can't. Artie drove me," she said, finally acknowledging him, still standing beside her, witnessing their reunion, "He has to get back to work."

Hearing this Artie intervened, "We can stay, mom. I can take the time, no problem."

Angela hesitated. "Are you sure?"

Margo knew her friend well enough to know it was probably a step too far for her to stay for lunch and mingle for an hour or two. Leaving was probably her preference. But Artie overrode her. He mouthed to Margo from above his mother's head, "We'll be there."

IN THE YEARS BEFORE KEVIN GOT SICK, THEIR DOCTOR suggested he and Margo complete a short document stating their last wishes. Questions included the desire for extraordinary measures to be taken in life-threatening situations, long term care, and final arrangements regarding burial and cremation. A gruesome task, when they finally got to it, they sat on opposite sides of the kitchen table, the basil blooming on the windowsill, sun flooding the room in light that would go on and on, even without them. They had chosen that morning to complete their task because they were both healthy, death seemed far away, and slender packets of questions were accumulating, since every time either of them went to the doctors for the slightest ailment, they returned with another packet. They didn't discuss their answers beforehand, but agreed to answer each question privately, and then compare their responses when finished. It went quickly. When they compared answers about their last wishes and desires, they found themselves in agreement on all but one, the final one. "What kind of funeral do you want?'

They both regressed to joking as they shared each other's response to the moment none can imagine—the world without us. Margo wrote "everyone should cry," and Kevin wrote, "have a party." Of course. They were both describing an aspect of an Irish wake where tears are mingled with laughter, tongues are loosened with alcohol, and stories told as the dead are remembered as though still alive.

Margo fulfilled Kevin's request. His repast was an upgraded version of an infamous Irish wake. The restaurant was prepared for them at noon. A buffet was set up under the windows streaming with midday sun. The road beyond was lined with trees stripped bare by autumn, reminding her of how empty her life was going to be. Platters of food, an open bar, and tables accommodating everyone were a reminder that even in dying, the living must go on.

Having taken care of some last-minute details with the funeral director, Margo was one of the last to arrive. The room seemed to be floating under water, a blur of color, like an abstract painting, as people merged into the furniture and each other. She took a deep breath and tried to refocus.

The tables, with their white tablecloths began to emerge like individual flowers from the depth of the watery background. It was then she saw Angela, her white suit haloed in the sunlight streaming through the window. Maura had just brought her a plate of food and was sitting down next to her at a table. Margo scanned the room to find Artie. In a far corner, she saw Finn and Artie in rapt conversation. She watched as they patted each other on the back in echoes of affection. The years dropped away in an exchange of business cards, but not before each pulled out a pen to add their private mobile numbers. They shook hands for a long time as they readied themselves to move on. Margo smiled and wondered if Kevin's death would be a new beginning for Finn and Artie, just as Lou's death had been for Angela and her. They had the rest of their lives to find out.

Thank you for reading *Hoops of Steel*. If you enjoyed the book, please leave a review or recommend it to a friend.

Made in the USA
Middletown, DE
10 October 2024

62419461R10154